THE FARO KID

Leslie Ernenwein was born in Oneida, New York. He began his newspaper career as a telegraph editor, but at eighteen went West where he rambled from Montana to Mexico, working as a cowboy and then as a freelance writer. In the mid 1930s he went back East to work for the *Schenectady Sun*. In 1938 he got a reporting position with the *Tucson Daily Citizen* and moved to Tucson permanently. Later that year he began writing Western fiction for pulp magazines, becoming a regular contributor to *Dime Western* and *Star Western*. His first Western novel, *Gunsmoke Galoot*, appeared in 1941, and was quickly followed by *Kinkade of Red Butte* and *Boss of Panamint* in 1942. In addition to publishing novels regularly, Ernenwein continued to contribute heavily to the magazine market, both Western fiction and factual articles. Among his finest work in the 1940s are *Rebels Ride Proudly* (1947) and *Rebel Yell* (1948), both dealing with the dislocations caused by the War Between the States. In the 1950s Ernenwein wrote primarily for original paperback publishers of Western fiction because the pay was better. *High Gun* in 1956, published by Fawcett Gold Medal, won a Spur Award from the Western Writers of America, the first original paperback Western to do so. That same year, since the pulp magazine market had all but vanished, Ernenwein returned to working for the Tucson Daily Citizen, this time as a columnist. Ernenwein's Western fiction may be broadly characterized as moral allegories, light against darkness, and at the center is a protagonist determined to fight against injustice before he is destroyed by it. *Bullet Barricade* (1955), perhaps his most notable novel from the 1950s, best articulates his vision of how the life of man is not governed by a fate over which he has no control, even though life itself may seem like a never-ending contest against moral evil.

THE FARO KID

Leslie Ernenwein

GUNSMOKE

This hardback edition 2009
by BBC Audiobooks Ltd
by arrangement with
Golden West Literary Agency

ISBN 978 1 405 68291 6

British Library Cataloguing in Publication Data available.

Printed and bound in Great Britain by
CPI Antony Rowe, Chippenham and Eastbourne

1

Twenty-seven days of steady riding brought Steve Rennevant to the crest of Cascabelle Divide an hour before sundown. There he halted, scouting the land ahead with the same deliberate attention for small details which had kept him close to the Faro Kid's heels all the way from Laramie.

Wind and sun and dust had honed Rennevant's face to the color of a rag-rubbed rosewood bar. It was a lean, rugged face with high cheek bones and broad lips and gently flaring nostrils. Long hair, showing shaggy black beneath his dust-peppered hat, merged with a two-day stubble of whiskers on his jaws. There was a searching eagerness in his gray eyes, and in the way he cocked his head—like a lobo questing for quarry.

A thousand miles northward men would tell you that Steve Rennevant was a lobo. They'd tell you he had killed upwards of a dozen men and that the gun he wore in a greased half-breed holster was dedicated to swift slaughter. But that was back in the railroad boomtown of Wyoming, and this was Arizona. Here, where jutting bastions towered above the sprawling breadth of Kettledrum Basin, Rennevant was unknown. Or so he thought. . . .

Garbed in the worn gear of a saddle tramp and carrying his deputy U. S. marshal badge deep in his pants pocket, Steve Rennevant didn't look like a lawman come to capture the Faro Kid, dead or alive. He looked like just another gun-hung drifter,

border-bound. The trail he'd followed so persistently
had petered out on this bald crest of black maplais,
but its loss was unimportant now. Heading south
after holding up a U. P. train single-handed, the
Faro Kid had never deviated from this one direction
during all the dusty miles Rennevant had trailed
him.

Gazing across Kettledrum Basin, Rennevant briefly
considered the distance-dwarfed huddle of houses
which was San Sabino. Then he estimated the miles
between that sun-hammered cow town and the hazy
hills which marked the Mexican border. No sign
showed against the tawny blanket of Border Desert;
no moving speck nor trailing plume of hoof-churned
dust. The Kid had been several hours in front all
the way from Wyoming, and it seemed certain that
he was across the line by now. A train-robbing
renegade wouldn't loiter this close to safety; he'd
slide into Sonora like a rat running for a hole.

With the logic of that shaping it into a definite
conclusion, Rennevant relaxed in the saddle. He
patted the sweat-crusted neck of his gib sorrel bronc
and said, self-mockingly, "Reckon we just came for
the ride, Rowdy hoss."

It was characteristic of Rennevant that he took
his failure with a gambler's fatalistic resignation.
Another man might have cursed and fumed at this
final frustration—might have shaken his fist at the
yonder blur of heat-hazed hills and vented his spite
by spurring his horse back up the trail toward home.
Especially a marshal who was proud of his man-
hunting prowess. And this Steve Rennevant was
proud. . . .

In the five years he'd worn a marshal's badge,
Rennevant had built himself a reputation. Starting
from scratch, with neither the background nor the
inclination of a gun fighter, he had practiced the

gunslick art hour on hour, day after day, until finally he had perfected a technique of drawing and firing that was one swift, perfectly coordinated motion.

There had been times during that period of practice when Rennevant had survived by feather-fine margins; one time in particular when only the split-second warning of a music-loving old gambler had saved him from certain death. But afterward, when the magic of his draw had become a legend along the Union Pacific, there'd been many times when he had deliberately taunted outlaws into grabbing guns. That was why men called him a killer; why they said he had a steel spring for a heart, and no mercy at all. Those men didn't know that Steve Rennevant's father had been butchered by bandits. They didn't know that a grief-stricken young cowpuncher had watched his father gasp out his life in gut-shot agony. And Rennevant had never bother to tell them why he hated holdup men with a hatred that was close to fanaticism.

Yet now, convinced that the Faro Kid had crossed into Mexico, Rennevant merely grinned his mirthless grin, and lifting a canteen, joggled it to appraise the amount of water it contained. A trivial thing, that gesture; just the small slosh of liquid in a half-filled canteen. But on it hung the destiny of men who'd never heard of Steve Rennevant. And one who had . . .

Finished with his estimate of the canteen's contents, Rennevant sat in reflective silence for a moment longer. There was, he judged, enough water to sustain him for the twenty miles north to the next water hole. His bronc could make it; but the animal would suffer. And Steve Rennevant had a lonely man's affection for his horse. Thus, ironically, it was a deep-rooted quality of kindness in Rennevant which sent him riding down the brush-tangled slants toward San Sabino—toward a holocaust of hate, greed and bushwhack bullets.

He had his first inkling of trouble when he started across the flats west of Cascabelle Divide. The bark of a distant gun shattered the silence with two shots in swift succession. Another gun blasted, and presently there were three spaced reports that sounded like long-range firing.

Rennevant halted his horse. He peered across the mesquite-dotted flats, searching for some telltale sign of powder smoke off to the west. But the sharp glare of the setting sun blinded his eyes and he was further handicapped by the remoteness of the shots. Shrugging off the unsolvable riddle of their exact location, he rode on and, quartering into a road at the entrance to a narrow pass, glimpsed a rider on its north wall.

This man sat tipped forward in the saddle, peering northward. A Winchester was cradled across his left arm and he wore a bone-handled Colt in a tied-down holster. For a moment, as Rennevant pulled up, the rider shifted his gaze as if undecided what course to take. Then, with a final glance northward, he sheathed the Winchester and slid his horse down the steep embankment.

Watching his hasty approach, Rennevant tried to tab the rider's age and breed—a lawman habit acquired by studying reward posters of wanted men. The stranger's blunt-featured face bore an old, ingrained viciousness, and his hair showed white where it bushed under the upcuffed brim of his hat; yet Rennevant guessed his age at not more than thirty-five.

The stranger rode up on Rennevant's right side, thus hiding his bronc's brand. Instantly resenting this lack of trail etiquette, Rennevant kneed his big sorrel into a step sideways and peered deliberately at the Double D brand on the stranger's bronc. When he glanced up he saw a vulpine suspiciousness in the man's amber eyes, and noticed the puckered scar of an old wound that made a round-nippled mound on his left cheek. There was something remotely familiar about that scar and about the man's dead-white hair . . .

"You hear some shootin'?" the stranger was asking. His voice had a brash, bullish tone that turned the question into a demand.

"Mebbe I did," Rennevant drawled, and knew abruptly why this man's face seemed familiar. There'd been a picture and a description of him on a Montana poster two years before—Whitey Hallmark, prematurely gray hair and a peculiar puckered scar on his left cheek—wanted for murder during a mail robbery.

"You just ridin' through?" Hallmark asked bluntly.

"Mebbe I am," Rennevant drawled again, with deceptive casualness, and nodded toward a plume of thunderheads above Cascabelle Divide. "Looks like we might get some rain."

Hallmark started to glance over his shoulder, decided against it, and eyed Rennevant warily. He had a furtive, uneasy way with him. The fingers of his right hand tinkered with the snub-nosed bullets in his gunbelt, and he kept shifting his weight in the saddle. Seeing this, and placing an accurate reckoning upon it, Rennevant laughed a little, deep inside. Hallmark was cocked for trouble; he was teetering on the thin edge of grabbing his gun!

"You got a hell of a way of answering questions," Hallmark accused him. "You ridin' through, or ain't you?"

There was no appreciable change in Rennevant's face, nor in his eyes, save for a slight deepening of the smoky blue that lurked behind their gray surfaces. But his voice carried a full cargo of arrogance when he said, "It's none of your goddam business!"

Hard on the heels of that declaration Rennevant jumped the sorrel ahead, wheeled in close to Hallmark and slapped his face.

Utter astonishment blanked Hallmark's features. His eyes bugged wide, and in that hushed interval all the cocked impatience left him. His right hand lifted to his cheek, fingering it in the dazed manner of a man not sure of his senses—like a man acting in a drunken stupor.

"What the hell!" he blurted as Rennevant kept urging the sorrel against his side-stepping bronc; kept crowding him across the road. "What the hell!"

Rage edged his voice now. A kind of sluggish, smouldering resentment mixed with astonishment. But after one hasty glance at Rennevant's hovering right hand, he lifted his own, shoulder high, and kept it there.

"What the hell you tryin' to do?" he demanded.

"I'm teaching you some proper manners," Rennevant said, and because this was a definite, long-practiced method of meeting toughness with toughness, he had a thorough confidence in what he was doing. Prod a rattlesnake long enough and hard enough—even a sluggish snake—and he'd finally get around to striking.

It occurred to Rennevant that there'd been other names on that old reward notice—three or four of them, all wanted for the same crime. He could prod Whitey into a shootout now, and be sure of killing one wanted thief; or he could ease off on him and gamble on a roundup. If the others were in Kettledrum Basin he'd have a chance to turn this trip into a real success, even though the Faro Kid had out-ridden him. . . .

Deciding to take the gamble, Rennevant inquired

tauntingly, "Any more questions you'd like to ask?"

Hallmark's face was wholly red now. His eyes had a feverish, glassy look, and the inward heat of his controlled rage spawned twin trickles of sweat that greased his cheeks. But he didn't speak—didn't voice the venom of his hate; he merely shook his head in sullen silence.

"Then vamose," Rennevant ordered gruffly.

Hallmark jabbed spurs to his horse. He went into the pass at a dust-boiling run, not glancing back.

Whereupon Rennevant grinned and drawled, "He spooked easy, didn't he, Rowdy hoss?"

Riding on through the pass, Rennevant watched Hallmark short-cut a wide bend in the road and presently disappear ahead of the sun-sparkled dust that trailed him. Why, Rennevant wondered, had Hallmark been waiting up there on the bluff with a Winchester in his hand?

Rennevant was still wondering about that, and the shots he'd heard, when he rode into San Sabino an hour later.

It was dusk now, and the town's lamplit doorways made broken patterns of alternate light and shadow across Main Street's wide dust. Three townsmen stood in front of Matabelle's Mercantile, silently watching a range-garbed rider go into the Border Belle Saloon, and the unswerving intensity of their watching pulled Rennevant's attention that way—to the old cowman going through the saloon's batwing gates. Rennevant had a fleeting glimpse of this man's face sharply etched in the doorway lamplight as he went on into the smoke-hazed room.

A dozen saddled horses stood in a hip-shot patience at the saloon hitchrack; beyond, in front of the San Sabino Bank, two ranch rigs were pulled up alongside the plank sidewalk. It occurred to Rennevant that the street was strangely quiet; that despite numerous groups of people standing about, no one was talking. They were all watching the saloon. Yet even then Rennevant had no real warning of the hell broth that was brewing in San Sabino. It was, he thought, just another cow town; just another collection of peeling old 'dobes and weather-warped frames sprawling between a cattle corral and a graveyard. For that was the pattern of these desert towns and it seldom varied, save in the size of their scatteration. But there was a difference here, and the sense of it was already nagging at the fringes of his mind.

Riding at a walk, Rennevant passed the Cattle King Hotel. A girl stood at the top of the veranda steps; a girl who was tall and blond and whose statuesque beauty was emphasized by the glow of lobby lamplight behind her. She wore a high-necked blouse that fitted snugly at the waist, and a blue velvet skirt that billowed out at its hem like a queenly robe. Something in the way she stood— with her hands clasped tightly between the twin mounds of her breasts—tinkled a bell in Rennevant's brain. She was peering at the saloon across the street with a strict and unwavering attention. Standing so, with the reflected glare of the saloon's chandeliers lighting her face, she was the living image of beauty in distress!

Rennevant had a curiously urgent impulse to halt his horse; to stop and ask this blond goddess of a girl what she was waiting for, and so plainly fearing. But she ignored his presence completely. Her attention remained focused on the yellow bloom of light spilling through the Border Belle's batwings; utterly absorbed in some repellent, yet compelling expectancy. It was as if she were hypnotized beyond the power of movement, as if her supple, shapely body were shackled to the veranda post against which she stood.

There was something downright peculiar about this town, Rennevant reflected. But there was no doubt in his mind about one part of the picture here. He had seen fear in too many faces to mistake it. The blond girl was afraid!

Going on along Main Street, Rennevant turned in at Hook Hooligan's Stable and looked at the one-handed oldster who stood directly beneath a doorway lantern. The liveryman had also been watching the Border Belle; he shifted his gaze now almost reluctantly.

Rennevant dismounted, slapped dust from his shirt and asked, "What's going on over there?"

"Unless I'm considerable mistook, 'tis the makin's of a suicide," Hooligan announced, as if voicing a conviction just forming in his mind. "And a pity it is."

Rennevant uncinched his saddle and, wondering if the Faro Kid had ridden through town on his way to the line, asked, "Did a youngish saddle tramp ride a blue roan bronc into town a little bit ago?"

"Nope," Hooligan replied without hesitation. Then, glancing at the brand on the sorrel's hip, he turned judging eyes on Rennevant's gun gear. "Ye ride in from the north?" he inquired.

Rennevant nodded. Whereupon Hook Hooligan, from long knowledge of backtrail riders and their ways, said, "Then ye won't be stayin' overnight."

It was, Rennevant understood, a reasonable conclusion. Border-bound drifters wouldn't stay long in San Sabino; just long enough to feed and water for the final run across the line. And because this wasn't the first time he'd been mistaken for a fiddlefooted renegade, Rennevant's lips loosened into a crooked grin. A man got to look like the riffraff he trailed, after a while; he even acted the same, always scouting the shadows and looking around corners and listening for stray sounds.

Lifting saddle and blanket to the kak pole, Rennevant sponged the sorrel's sweat-soaked back, a strict habit that had saved Rowdy from saddle sores despite long and hard riding. "Give him a double ration of oats and all the clean hay he'll eat," he ordered. "I'm staying overnight."

The surprise caused by that showed instantly in Hooligan's ape-featured face. It hoisted his shaggy eyebrows and brightened his faded blue eyes. "Then ye must be signin' on with the Double D," he said probingly.

Rennevant shook his head. "Never heard of it," he drawled.

The liveryman seemed entirely puzzled. "Ye niver heered of the Double D, and ye ain't high-tailin' south," he speculated in the fashion of a man listing the facts of a tricky riddle. Then a new thought struck him, and he asked, "Ye wouldn't be some friend of Bob Cruzatte, now would ye?"

"No," Rennevant said, "Who's Bob Cruzatte?"

"The son of Jeff Cruzatte, who owns the big Anvil spread, or what's left of it. Young Bob was supposed to be bringin' home money so's Jeff could hire a fightin' crew to buck the Double D. But Bob ain't showed up yit."

Recalling the shots out on the mesquite flats, Rennevant had a hunch they were somehow connected with Bob Cruzatte's failure to reach San Sabino. But he had no premonition of the role Fate was already fashioning for him in this game of guns and greed and watching men. . . .

"That was Jeff Cruzatte just went into the Border Belle," Hooligan explained. "Unless I'm considerable mistook he won't come out alive."

"Why not?" Rennevant inquired.

Hooligan snaked up Rowdy's reins with the steel hook which served him for a right hand. He studied Rennevant's face for a brief interval, then said slyly, "Mebbe ye ain't heered of the Double D, but I'm bettin' ye've heered of Diamond Dan Bannerman, which is the same thing. So I'm lettin' ye dig yer own onions, bejasus!"

And with that ultimatum, Hook Hooligan led Rowdy back into the barn.

Rennevant shrugged and, sauntering leisurely along Main Street, passed a barbership where two men stood in the doorway. One of them held a razor in his right hand; the other's face was lathered for shaving. They were both looking toward the saloon. . . .

San Sabino, Rennevant reflected, had a familiar feel to it. This town made him remember a town in Texas when the roundabout country had been clutched in the grip of range war. That town had turned into a place of fear, of furtive watching and hushed waiting; it had held the same sense of brooding expectancy. He sent a roving glance along Main Street, contemplating its lamplit windows—probing its shadows. Purely a routine gesture, this scrutiny; the strict habit of a man long trained to seek answers in obscure places.

North of Main Street, and high enough above it so that their lights showed over the roofs of buildings there, a half dozen houses perched proudly on the brow of a hill. That, Rennevant guessed, would be the respectable part of town; a sort of reserved section for citizens of social standing and financial stability. The pattern never varied much. Abilene, Coffeyville, Dodge City—all had their select minority, their genteel carriage trade hoisting its skirts away from the unlovely source of its income.

When Rennevant came abreast of Estevan's Cafe,

the fine fragrance of boiling coffee reminded him that he hadn't eaten since sunup. Halting there, he saw that the blond girl still stood on the hotel veranda. From this distance her face was little more than an oval shadow, yet her presence pulled at him like a plucking hand. It was a peculiar thing. A disturbing thing. He had known his share of women; some good, some bad, some almost beautiful. But he was no part of a calico chaser, and this girl's attraction puzzled him.

A warm breeze, carrying a hint of rain, drifted down from the north hills. It stirred dust fumaroles in the street and brought the smell of coffee more strongly to Rennevant's nostrils. Abruptly then he was hungry, eager to sample town cooking after days of saddle-pocket scraps. Discarding a desire to see the blond girl at closer quarters, he turned into the restaurant doorway and stopped briefly, giving the box-like room a quick appraisal.

One man occupied a stool at the counter. His back was turned to Rennevant, but there was something familiar about this man's slightly battered stovepipe hat and the way his narrow shoulders hunched forward, as if warped by long sitting. For a dozen seconds Rennevant tried to identify him—to decide which of the many tinhorns he'd met, this man might be. Some of those meetings had not been pleasant, and because a familiar face often meant meeting an enemy, Rennevant's eyes turned wary as he walked to the counter.

Choosing a stool to the left of the cafe's lone customer, Rennevant sat down and had his first view of the man's face. For a moment then, as the other turned toward him, neither of them spoke. They sat stiffly alert, coldly appraising, in the manner of strange dogs with raised hackles.

Little Lon Estevan came out of the kitchen, wip-

ing his flour-dusted hands on a sugar-sack apron.
"T-bone steak, fried spuds veree nice," he said
meekly, and stood poised as if for instant flight.
"You want heem?"

Rennevant nodded, not shifting his gaze from the
chalky-cheeked old man in the shabby black coat.
Then a low whistle slid from his lips and he said
gustily, "Piano Pete Modesto!"

A quick smile eased Modesto's bony, high-beaked
face. He stuck out a scrawny hand and exclaimed,
"You've changed, friend Steve. You look ten years
older."

"I don't like to think how I'd look if you hadn't
yelled at me that night in Cheyenne," Rennevant
declared, and gave Modesto's fragile fingers a grip
that made the gambler wince. "I'd of been buzzard
bait, sure enough, except for you, Pete."

Then he asked, "What you doing down here in
the desert?"

The smile faded from Modesto's gaunt face. He
tapped his chest, and said dismally, "I took t.b. that
last winter in Wyoming. Damn near died. Medicos
said this climate was my only chance."

"Working here?" Rennevant inquired.

Something like shame shadowed Modesto's glassy,
too bright eyes. He sent a hasty glance over his
shoulder, then spoke in that toneless murmur of men
to whom breath is a priceless commodity. "I'm dealing cards for the biggest crook in Arizona Territory,"
he said. "I used to deal off the top of the deck, Steve.
You know that. But not now. Not when I'm dealing
for Diamond Dan Bannerman. He's the greediest
galoot God ever let live, and he's got me gimmicked.
I've got to stay here, or croak, so I'm dealing the way
Bannerman orders."

"A hell of a way to earn a living," Rennevant reflected.

Modesto shrugged, and said glumly, "Croaking with t.b. is a hell of a way of dying."

Estevan brought Rennevant's meal and scurried back to the kitchen like a spooked jackrabbit. Whereupon Rennevant asked, "What's wrong with this town, Pete? Everyone acts like they got ticks in their britches."

"That," Modesto muttered, "is the Bannerman influence."

"Must be a right salty gink, this Bannerman."

"He's the nearest thing to a brass-riveted king you ever saw, Steve. He owns the Border Belle Saloon and the Double D ranch, controls county politics and uses the law for a front. Only one man had the guts to buck Bannerman, and he went bankrupt doing it."

"Jeff Cruzatte?" Rennevant asked.

Modesto nodded. "Old Jeff used to be the big mogul in this country. His riding crews elected sheriffs, his payrolls supported the stores, and his daughter set the style for this whole end of Arizona. But four dry years in a row put the skids under Cruzatte; his credit had run out at the bank when Bannerman moved in and bought out two of Jeff's neighbors at poverty prices. Bannerman made quite a play for Jeff's daughter, and offered to buy a half interest in the Anvil. But he got turned down both ways, and there's been trouble between the two outfits ever since."

Rennevant asked casually, "Is Cruzatte's daughter tall and blond?"

"That's her," Piano Pete said, "Anne Cruzatte—pretty as a picture and proud as a queen. Well, like I was saying, Diamond Dan couldn't bribe Cruzatte and he couldn't bluff him. But the old man had one weakness: he liked to buck the tiger. And he couldn't afford to lose. It took crooked cards to beat him, which is why I'm feeling lower than snake sign in a wheel rut, friend Steve. I dealt the cards."

"So?" Rennevant mused. "Well, Cruzatte don't seem to know when he's licked. He went into the Border Belle a few minutes ago."

Piano Pete slid from his stool. "Jeff won't have a prayer, if he starts anything!" he exclaimed. "And it'll only take about four drinks to set him off!"

Then he glanced sharply at Rennevant, as if remembering something important; something that might make a difference. "You were plenty fast with a gun when I left Wyoming," he said thoughtfully. "How are you now?"

"Fair," Rennevant admitted. "Why?"

Two scarlet spots stained Modesto's cheeks and his cavernous eyes glowed like burning coals. "I'm asking you a favor," he said, his voice showing the stress of mounting excitement. "Get Cruzatte out of the Border Belle alive!"

2

RENNEVANT laid down his fork. He eyed Modesto narrowly. "What's your payoff in this game?" he asked.

"One you'd never guess," the gambler muttered. "How about the favor, Steve?"

"Well, I owe you one. But I'm not exactly looking for trouble, Pete. I'm no smokeroo."

"You were the next thing to it, last time we met," Modesto declared. "You killed two men in less than a minute, friend Steve. You killed them cold turkey, and deader than hell."

So that was it. This reedy old card shark was remembering that night in Cheyenne. And because it had been the ultimate test of his patient practicing, Steve Rennevant remembered it, too. All the rest of his life he would remember it. . . .

He could recall each detail, even to the cold rain that had turned Cheyenne into a hoof-pocked, wheel-churned mud hole. Eddy Street jammed with creaking freight wagons; men of all colors and all creeds crowding stores, saloons and dance halls. The Union Pacific had just run its rails west from Omaha and Cheyenne was riding the crest of a boom. In that hurdy-gurdy confusion of wild Irish railroaders, money-mad merchants, gamblers and painted percentage girls stood a young deputy marshal come to preserve law and order; a marshall not quite sure of his gun skill, nor of his nerve.

"You can save Cruzatte," Modesto urged eagerly. "With that fast draw of yours you might not need to fire a shot. Just go in there and keep them from hoorawing him into a fight."

But Rennevant wasn't listening. He was remembering that night in Cheyenne, with every saloon and gambling joint packed to the doors—every dance hall and bawdy house running full blast. The show-down had come at the Cross Tie Cafe, and the memory of it now flashed vividly across the mirrors of his mind. Late at night it was, with Pete Modesto sitting at the piano playing *Black-Eyed Susie* in a way that made a man remember better days and pleasanter ways. There'd been a sudden flurry of oaths at a poker table—a player's rash protest and then a gambler's derringer blasting the player down. The young marshal had foolishly rushed to the table without drawing his gun, and was strong-arming the gambler out of the place when Piano Pete called: "Lawdog—look out!"

Those next few seconds were sharply etched in Rennevant's memory. . . . The fleeting glimpse of an uptilting gun . . . his mind registering the unalterable fact that he had to draw fast enough to beat that gun at the bar, or die. The rest of it had been automatic, without conscious thought or volition. He'd drawn and fired—fast. Faster than ever before. And when that yonder gunman staggered back against the bar, Rennevant had whirled and fired again, fast enough to beat out the gambler he'd arrested. Long, tedious training had made him good with a gun; but it was the call of a piano-playing card shark that saved his life.

Now Pete Modesto was thinking that the kid marshal of that night had developed into a free-lance gunhawk; that he'd joined the grisly brotherhood of professional killers who sold their skill to the highest bidder. And Modesto was bidding high—was holding him to the killer's creed of a life for a life.

"What about Cruzatte's crew?" Rennevant asked. "Can't they get him out of there?"

"He's got no crew left," Modesto said. He went to the door, glanced apprehensively along the street and came directly back to the counter. "How about it?" he demanded.

It occurred to Rennevant that he could produce his marshal badge and show this conscience-stricken gambler why he couldn't get mixed up in a private shooting scrape. Deputy U.S. marshals were allowed considerable leeway, especially roving manhunters whose only barriers were the two borders, Mexican and Canadian. But that leeway didn't permit a marshal to use his gun in payment of a personal debt —even though he owed his life on that debt.

"I've got my reasons for not wanting chips in the game here," he said, and felt for the badge in his pocket.

Modesto made an open-palmed gesture with hands that were slim and soft as a woman's hands that could caress piano keys into sweet music, or slip aces from the bottom of a deck. The typical hands of a tin-horn gambler. Yet now, with that shadow of shame burned out of his eyes by some deeper, stronger emotion, Piano Pete didn't look like a tin-horn. He looked like an old man haunted by the ghosts of lost yesterdays. And so he was. . . .

"Never did much gun work," he muttered. "Didn't need to, when I was dealing them straight. But I'll make a try, if you'll lend me your gun."

That did it. That, and the beaten expression in Modesto's too bright eyes. Rennevant's fingers released the badge—let it drop back into his pocket without being seen. And because there was a deep-rooted sense of humor in him, he laughed a little as he got to his feet. The angles of this play made a crazy-quilt pattern. A gambler had saved the life of a lawman; now the gambler was asking that lawman to risk his life for the man Modesto had cheated into bankruptcy. And the gambler had turned to crooked cards so that he might keep the breath of life in his disease-wasted body. Fate, Rennevant reflected, couldn't possibly have packed more twists into the payoff of one debt.

But Steve Rennevant was wrong about that, and would soon know it. . . .

He said, "I'll take a whirl at your Good Samaritan game."

Modesto's hollow cheeks creased into a quick smile. "Good!" he exclaimed. "Good!"

"What'll I be up against over in the saloon?"

"Can't say for sure," Modesto admitted. "There was a meeting of the Homestead Hills Pool this afternoon, so I suppose there'll be a crowd in the Border Belle. But the Pool members are just a bunch of two-bit cowmen who owe the bank their shirts. Jeff tried to talk them into a showdown fight against the Double D six months ago when he had a crew to throw in with them. But they turned him down."

The old gambler took a drink of water and added hurriedly, "Whitey Hallmark, Bannerman's foreman, rode in about sundown. Two more Double D riders —Turk Gallego and Red Haggin—came into town a few minutes ago. They'll be over there with Bannerman, along with Sheriff Shumway, who is Diamond Dan's personal errand boy."

"I met Whitey Hallmark out on the stage road," Rennevant muttered, wondering if the other two were wanted men, hoping that they were.

"Gallego is a newcomer," Modesto said. "He's short and dark and looks tough as Texas whang, but Haggin is the one you want to watch. He's shifty as a snake and kill-crazy to boot."

Rennevant took out his gun, examined the loads and slid it into holster. "Sounds like a real nice party," he drawled. "It does for a fact."

He went over to the door, and when Modesto moved to accompany him, Rennevant said, "You'd be no help without a gun."

"I was that night in Cheyenne," Piano Pete reminded him.

Rennevant motioned him back. "I've learned to keep my eyes peeled since then," he said. "You stay here and shoo flies off my steak. I'll be back to finish it."

And stepping out to the sidewalk, he added, "Mebbe."

A spacious room at the rear of the Border Belle Saloon served Diamond Dan Bannerman as office and living quarters when he was in town, which was frequently.

Big and bull-bodied, Bannerman now sat in his high-back swivel chair as a king might sit on a throne. Somewhere in his middle thirties, he was a man of strange contrasts. Bald, save for a sorrel fringe that circled the dome of his massive head like a loose-fitting crown, he had eyebrows that made a bushy, unbroken hedge above green-gray eyes, and his mustache was thick as the roached mane of a horse. There was contrast, too, in the way he dressed. His white shirt was soiled at the collar and the starched cuffs were rimmed with grime, yet he wore the black broadcloth of a fashionable townsman; a diamond-studded pin in his silk tie was fashioned into a Double D brand, and he wore the scuffed boots of a brush-popping cowpuncher.

Those boots rested now on the top of a scarred mahogany desk, and their back-tilted owner was eyeing Sheriff Fay Shumway, who stood just inside the closed door. "So Cruzatte wants to see me," Bannerman muttered.

Shumway was also built of generous proportions. But he was cut from a different pattern. Where Diamond Dan gave the impression of solid beef—of enormous power and energy—Shumway was merely fat. His round, spongy face was mottled and his toady eyes were set too close to a bulbous, whiskey-reddened nose.

"Cruzatte," the sheriff reported, "is calling you names. He's saying your dealer cold-decked him out of his bankroll."

He loosed a cackling laugh and added, "You wouldn't let no such outrage be committed in your place, now would you, Dan?"

"If he thinks that, why don't he talk to Piano Pete?" Bannerman inquired.

"Says Pete was just following your orders, and he ain't fighting no invalid."

Bannerman chuckled. "Cruzatte will have a tough time proving I gave the orders, unless Modesto talks. And I don't think the old tinhorn will do much talking. He's a trifle short of breath."

"Proof or not, Cruzatte is yelling it around," the sheriff said doggedly. "And he's saying your riders shoved a big bunch of Double D steers onto his range last night—after ripping out a long section of his drift fence. You want me to throw the old hellion out into the street?"

Diamond Dan considered that question with squinting thoughtfulness. Predatory, proud of his growing power, and unfettered by any rule save the jungle law of survival, he had accomplished most of the many things he'd set out to do when he first came to Kettledrum Basin. A long drought had brought the whole range to the ragged edge of ruin; the cowmen were all broke and the San Sabino Bank was over-loaned to the point of actual insolvency. There'd been all kinds of opportunities for a man with money. And he'd had cash aplenty.

Recalling his conquests, Diamond Dan smiled. Most of them had been easy. Just a matter of money. All except one. And thinking of that one now, he ceased smiling. At first he'd been confident that the threat of bloody conflict would be sufficient—that the one prize he sought above all others could be won by a strong bluff of range war. When that had failed, he'd used the pressure of impending poverty. But the prize still evaded him, and Dan Bannerman had a proud man's dislike for failure. . . .

He held up his right hand, turning it so that the huge diamond on his little finger caught the glow of the bracket lamp above him. The stone's facets threw off a blue-white brilliance that made a brittle glint against his considering eyes. "Beautiful," he mused. "Beautiful as a blond woman."

"And just as cold," Shumway said dryly. "Don't look like you'll ever thaw her out, Dan."

Swift anger glinted in Bannerman's eyes. "I'll get her," he muttered flatly. "One way or another, I'll get her. Before I'm done with this country she'll come begging for a bed to sleep in. Any kind of bed at all!"

Then he said, "Once I crowd Cruzatte off the Anvil, I'll control this end of Arizona, Fay. And you know what that means. Big money. Fast money. I'll own the bank and control every business in town. But I've got to have the Anvil first."

"You going to turn Red Haggin loose on Cruzatte?" Shumway asked.

"No, I've got a better idea. We'll give the old buzzard time to take on a couple more drinks, and get his dander up. Then I'll come out and hear what he's got to say."

"He's sore as a bull with a busted horn," Shumway warned. "He's talking showdown tonight, regardless."

"That's fine," Bannerman declared. "And that's where you come into the picture, Fay. Being sheriff, it's your sworn duty to protect life and property at all times. Especially mine. If Cruzatte makes a play, you cut him down—legally."

"You think he'll grab a gun?" Shumway asked.

"I'll guarantee it," Bannerman bragged.

It wasn't far from Estevan's Cafe to the Border Belle Saloon; less than twice the width of Main Street. Yet in the few seconds it took him to pass the unlighted San Sabino Bank and cross the alley beyond it, Steve Rennevant's mind registered many sharp impressions.

There was another girl on the Cattle King veranda. She stood close to Anne Cruzatte, a small, dark-

haired girl wearing a flowered calico dress. Rennevant saw her glance run on beyond him. She, too, he
guessed, was watching for someone. Shifting his
glance to Anne Cruzatte, he recalled Modesto's
highly descriptive words—"pretty as a picture, proud
as a queen."

Several men stood in front of Matabelle's Mercantile now. Beyond them another man moved in-
distinctly down the middle of the unlighted street.
The pungent odor of wet greasewood drifted in from
the flats, and because all his boyhood had been spent
with cattle, Rennevant took a cowman's satisfaction
in the knowledge that it would soon be raining here.
When he stepped up to the saloon stoop he glanced
toward the livery's lantern-lit doorway and saw Hook
Hooligan perched on his bench, stolidly watching.
And in that moment, as the taint of tobacco smoke
and stale whiskey drifted out to him, Rennevant
realized that the Border Belle was ominously quiet.
The whole town was gripped in a brittle, breathless
hush—waiting and watching; filled with a grim premonition of things to come.

Rennevant nudged his gun loose in its leather. He
stepped to the batwing gates and stood there long
enough to let his eyes focus in accommodation to
the inside light. There were, he noticed, two massive
chandeliers suspended from the ceiling; but only the
front one was lighted.

Six range-garbed men stood at the bar, behind
which was a big-bellied man with scanty hair combed
crossways on his nearly bald head. None of those
men were drinking, or talking; they were all looking
toward the rear of the long, smoke-fogged room.

Glancing quickly that way, Rennevant saw Whitey
Hallmark standing near a big man whom he identi-
fied as Diamond Dan Bannerman by the twin glitter
of pin and ring. Near them, to the right, was a fat

man with a star on his vest; farther back and on the other side, a lathy, dark-faced little rider leaned indolently against the rear wall. Remembering the names Modesto had mentioned, Rennevant tallied these two as Sheriff Shumway and Turk Gallego. Midway between the bar and Bannerman, Jeff Cruzatte stood weaving on wide-propped feet. . . .

This much Rennevant saw as he pushed through the swinging gates. The thought came to him that he had seen this picture before, at many times and in many places. It was plain as hoof prints in the dust, as dismal as the repetition of an old and humorless joke. One man caught in the web of his own rashness; one man against four, with a crowd morbidly watching and waiting.

Lamplight put a ruddy shine on the solid planes of Bannerman's face, deepening the ruts that creased his heavy cheeks. He said, "You are a poor sport, Cruzatte. Your luck was bad and you lost. Now you're squawking like an old woman at camp meeting!"

Easing along the side wall, Rennevant heard Cruzatte exclaim, "Mebbeso, Bannerman. Mebbe my luck was bad. But luck didn't rip down my drift fence, and it didn't push upwards of five hundred Double D steers onto my grass last night!"

Rennevant's unnoticed advance gave him a view of the Anvil's owner. Cruzatte, he decided at once, wasn't any part of a gambler. His hawk-beaked face and faded eyes showed too much of his feelings. Because Rennevant's father had been a member of this outspoken, hell-for-leather breed of cowman, he felt sorry for Jeff Cruzatte. They made good pioneers, these arrogant old warriors; but they were no match for the crafty connivers who always followed the trails they blazed. . . .

A slyly taunting note came into Bannerman's

voice. "You used to be top dog in this country, Cruzatte. But you lost your bite, and your bark don't mean much any more. So quit your goddam barking. I've got no time to waste with bad loosers."

"It won't take a minute," Cruzatte said rashly. "And only one bullet!"

A man at the bar called, "Take it easy, Jeff—take it easy!"

He took a step forward, as if on the verge of siding Cruzatte. But the old cowman growled, "You keep out of this, Larson. I want no truck with your two-bit bunch, none at all!"

Then his big-knuckled fingers splayed close to the holstered gun at his hip and he blurted, "Drag iron, Bannerman!"

Diamond Dan's glance shifted swiftly from Cruzatte to Sheriff Shumway. It was a fleeting thing, that glance, accomplished without moving his head. But fast as it was, Rennevant saw it—and understood instantly how this game was to be played. The sheriff's tallow-white hand slid closer to his gun butt; Turk Gallego visibly straightened; and Hallmark stepped quickly to the left.

Bannerman was still faintly smiling; still playing his slick role for the men at the bar. And because Rennevant had seen this trick played before, he guessed instantly that Dan Bannerman was unarmed. In which event the big man had it framed perfectly. With Shumway all cocked for the kill, Bannerman was taunting the drink-dazed old cowman into grabbing his gun. Then the sheriff would kill Cruzatte.

As simply and brutally as that it would be done. And it would be entirely legal, if Bannerman was unarmed. No court in cattleland would question the killing of a man who had drawn a gun against an unarmed adversary. Or attempted to draw one . . .

For fleeting seconds no one moved and no one spoke. The silence got thinner and thinner. It was like the last frayed strand of a breaking rope. Expectancy flowed through the long room, the sense of it so strong that men held their breath.

One of the men at the bar said worriedly, "Wait, Jeff. We'll help you fix that busted drift fence."

Cruzatte shook his head, and said stubbornly, "I been waitin' too goddam long, Highbaugh. Waitin' for you fools to wake up. Now I'm goin' it alone!"

But he didn't draw, and because Steve Rennevant wanted no part of the deal, his mind grasped at a flimsy straw. This talking and waiting might crack Jeff Cruzatte's courage—might drive a wedge of caution into his whiskey-flared anger. A blind man should have recognized how this thing was rigged— and how it would end.

That frugal hope was building into a conviction, when Dan Bannerman moved. The big man's right hand pushed back the flowing folds of his black coat with a plain, almost leisurely gesture. Seeing the start of that, and of Cruzatte's fumbling draw, Rennevant jumped across to Cruzatte, and slammed into the old cowman with an impact that drove him back toward the bar.

All this in the time it took Sheriff Shumway to snake up his gun. The big-bellied lawman stood now with bafflement loosening his gross features. When Rennevant glanced at Dan Bannerman he saw what he had expected to see: Diamond Dan hadn't drawn a gun; he had pulled a white handkerchief from his hip pocket!

Jeff Cruzatte demanded dazedly: "Who are you?"

But Rennevant ignored him. He watched anger and disappointment merge into a scowl of plain puzzlement on Bannerman's face. Then, as Bannerman shoved the handkerchief back into his pocket, a startled scream lanced in from the street. And at that same moment another feminine voice called: "Dad—Bob is here!"

That seemed to sober Jeff Cruzatte instantly. "Thank God!" he exclaimed, and strode hurriedly toward the doorway.

The men at the bar shuffled uneasily, the portent of those outside voices plainly pulling at their interest. When one of them wheeled abruptly toward the door, the others followed, and the fat barkeep waddled after them. Rennevant heard their departure, but he didn't see it. He was watching Bannerman, seeing the bafflement in this man's eyes as Diamond Dan stared at Turk Gallego.

Sheriff Shumway holstered his gun. He, too, stared questioningly at Gallego, and so did Whitey Hallmark. Watching this shift of attention and guessing what lay behind it, Rennevant had his first full look at Gallego. The Double D rider was relaxed again; he leaned indolently against the wall, a lantern-jawed little man with a body thin as a rail.

"So Bob Cruzatte has arrived," Bannerman said in a voice barbed with accusation.

Rennevant's mind registered the quick conviction that Bannerman had ordered his riders to ambush young Cruzatte, and Gallego had somehow failed in following those orders. Now the Double D boss was wondering how Cruzatte had come through a blockade which had probably been set for days. . . .

Gallego's lean cheeks didn't change. But his eyes took on a glint that turned them brittle as broken glass. He nodded toward Rennevant and asked flatly, "What's he doing here?"

That question switched the focus of attention instantly. And it showed Rennevant how sharp a mind this dark-faced rider possessed. The other three men had been stampeded by Anne Cruzatte's words;

they'd been so surprised they'd forgotten his presence there. But not Turk Gallego.

Bannerman peered at Rennevant with deliberate appraisal. "What's your business in this town?" he demanded.

Rennevant dug a sack of Durham from his shirt pocket. He shaped up a cigarette with exaggerated care, letting the silence ride on for a full moment before he spoke. Then he thumbnailed a match. "My business wouldn't interest you," he drawled, and lit his cigarette.

"The hell it wouldn't!" Bannerman exclaimed irritably. "What you doing in San Sabino?"

"Smoking a cigarette," Rennevant said, and backed that explanation by exhaling a deep drag of smoke that reached Dan Bannerman's face.

Anger painted the big man's cheeks a deeper hue. But his voice showed the quick change in his thinking. "So you're tough," he muttered. "Well, maybe the sheriff here might take a notion to find out what your business is. There's no welcome sign for smokeroos hanging at our town limits."

"No?" Rennevant mused, glanced deliberately at Whitey Hallmark. "When did you take it down?"

Sheriff Shumway stepped forward in the hesitant fashion of a man compelled to make a show, and not relishing the chore. "That kind of talk won't do you no good," he declared, and tapped the star on his vest. "I'm the law here, and I'm taking you in."

"What for?" Rennevant inquired with deceiving gentleness.

That simple question seemed to stump Sheriff Shumway. He glanced at Bannerman as if wanting instructions. In this hushed interval Turk Gallego built a cigarette, tapering it with such exacting care that not a single crumb of tobacco fell from the paper. It was, Rennevant guessed, a tip off to Turk's character; it went with his tight eyes and the bachelor patches on his scabby chaps. By every indication Gallego was a frugal man who wouldn't waste words—or bullets.

Shumway said finally, "I'm arresting you on suspicion."

"Of what?" Rennevant asked, his voice still mildly casual.

Again Sheriff Shumway glanced at Bannerman. But the big man made no suggestion; he just stood there eyeing Rennevant in the judging way a cattle buyer might look at a prize bull.

"There's been some rustling hereabouts lately," Shumway declared. "I'm arresting you for that."

"A fake charge," Rennevant said, "from a fake lawdog."

"You're under arrest!" Shumway thundered, and grabbed for his gun. But he didn't draw it. He took one squinting look at Rennevant's uptilting gun and took his hand away from his holster.

Rennevant grinned, and said chidingly, "One of these days you'll get yourself hurt, bluffing like that."

Shumway's lips went thin with the pressure of his rage; thin and vicious, matching the wicked glint in his narrowed eyes. Rennevant laughed with real enjoyment now, for next to killer thieves, he hated political lawmen who made a mockery of the badge they wore.

"I don't reckon you want to arrest me," he drawled, and backed toward the doorway, keeping Gallego and Hallmark in the fringe of his vision. They wouldn't be foolish enough to buck a drawn gun, and Banerman was unarmed. Shumway looked furious enough to do almost anything right now, but he was a shameless politician, and wouldn't risk his hide at these odds. . . .

Dan Bannerman said arrogantly, "When you reach the street, keep going, stranger."

"Mebbe yes—mebbe no," Rennevant drawled.

Then, as he saw the furtive shift of Shumway's eyes and heard a batwing gate creak behind him Rennevant realized that someone was easing into the saloon—someone moving so stealthily that no footsteps sounded!

The bartender, he thought fleetingly. The fat-faced, thin-haired slob who stood behind the bar. He cocked his head, tautly listening. A wordless drone of excited voices drifted in from the street. But although the sense of someone behind him made his shoulder muscles crawl, he could detect no sound of movement.

A secretive smile loosened Dan Bannerman's broad lips. Sheriff Shumway's eyes took on a hot glint, and Hallmark began fingering the shells in his gun belt. Turk Gallego, finished with shaping his cigarette, held an unlighted match half raised in his right hand.

Then Rennevant's ears picked up the faint, scarcely audible tinkle of a spur rowel—and knew instantly it wasn't the barkeep behind him!

Hard on the heels of that came a startling recollection of Piano Pete's remark about Red Haggin. "Shifty as a snake, and kill-crazy to boot!" the old gambler had warned him.

3

PIANO PETE Modesto didn't follow Steve Rennevant's instructions to shoo flies from his steak. Instead he

stepped out to the restaurant stoop and watched Rennevant go into the Border Belle Saloon.

For several minutes then, Modesto waited. He
glanced frequently at the Cattle King veranda where
Kate Carmody stood with Anne Cruzatte; he recognized Doc Dineen and Mayor Matabelle in the group
that stood in front of the Mercantile, and was remotely aware of a man walking just beyond them.
But his chief attention was centered on the saloon.

Presently Hook Hooligan sauntered up from the
livery and asked: "Who's that coming down the
middle of the street?"

"It looks like too much mescal on the hoof," Modesto muttered, and saw the man collapse in front
of the Mercantile.

Then Doc Dineen exclaimed, "He's shot! He's shot
to doll ribbons!"

The two girls hurried down the hotel steps, and
Hook Hooligan asked again, "Who the hell is it,
Pete?"

Modesto was wondering that same thing, when
Kate Carmody's scream lanced along the street. Instantly then he guessed the man's identity.

"It's Bob Cruzatte," he declared, and heard Anne
verify his instinctive guess by calling to her father.

Hooligan ran along the sidewalk. Jeff Cruzatte
came barging through the saloon batwings and men
rushed from a dozen doorways. But Rennevant didn't
come out of the saloon, and that fact stirred quick
apprehension in Modesto. Then he saw Red Haggin
step up to the saloon stoop—saw him peer over the
batwings and draw his gun!

Modesto loosed a sighing curse and, walking faster
than he'd walked in many months, went to Border
Belle Alley which ran alongside the saloon. Over in
the street Doc Dineen was saying, "Carry him into

the hotel and be careful. He's lost too much blood already."

Piano Pete was strongly aware of Kate Carmody's low sobbing; of Anne Cruzatte's emotion throbbing voice giving instructions, and old Jeff saying, "The dirty, stinkin' sons," over and over. But because Red Haggin was now easing through the batwings, Modesto paid the crowd no heed. He turned into the dark alley and, halting near an open window on the saloon's side wall, glimpsed Steve Rennevant standing with his back to the doorway.

Whereupon Modesto took a heavy, stem-winding watch from his vest pocket, hefting it as a man might heft a stone for throwing. And at that exact moment Red Haggin ordered gruffly, "Drop your smokepole, stranger—drop it quick!"

Hearing that command, and guessing who had uttered it, Steve Rennevant stood rigidly poised. Turk Gallego still held the raised match in his right hand. Now he snapped the match into flame, held it to his cigarette and, inhaling deeply, allowed the smoke to filter leisurely from his nostrils. His swarthy face was entirely impassive.

But the faces of Bannerman and Shumway and Hallmark weren't impassive. They were loosely smiling, filled with eager anticipation. Rennevant's down-tilted gun still menaced them, and so they made no move, but Shumway declared gloatingly, "Reckon you won't be so goddam tough now, feller. You won't be tough at all when we git through with you!"

"He sure needs dressin' down!" Whitey Hallmark exclaimed, grinning wickedly. "He needs guttin' with a dull knife."

Then Red Haggin snarled, "Drop that gun—or I'll blow your backbone clean through your belly!"

"Go ahead," Rennevant muttered, aiming his big

.44 at Bannerman's belt buckle. "I'll have company when I go."

There wasn't much of a chance here, he knew grimly. Just a jump-and-shoot play that would allow a man to die as he'd lived—with a blazing gun in his hand. Yet, because he had a strongly fatalistic streak in him, Steve Rennevant accepted the odds without question, and without regret. For any kind of a gamble was better than being butchered like a chute-trapped steer. And that's what surrender would bring him—sure, swift slaughter. It showed in Bannerman's loose-lipped smile, in Shumway's hot eyes and in the way Hallmark was tinkering with the bullets in his belt.

A mirthless grin quirked Rennevant's lips and toughness turned his eyes a smoky blue. The thought flashed through his mind that this was like that night in Cheyenne when Piano Pete had yelled at him. The faces here were different and the names were different; but the odds were about the same. Recognition of that fact quickened his pulse. A thin, wild hope of survival came to him; all his senses sharpened and the instinct for self-preservation was like strong wine in his veins.

"Better do like Red says," Bannerman advised in a mocking, satin-smooth voice. "He ain't fooling."

"Neither am I," Rennevant said flatly, keeping Bannerman covered.

But he knew it was just a question of time until Haggin got close enough to jump him from behind, or Bannerman ducked sideways—or Whitey Hallmark gambled on a sneak draw. A man couldn't cover all the angles here with one gun, no matter how fast he was!

Then, as Rennevant tensed his muscles for a fast step sideways and a whirling shot at Haggin, something brightly golden sailed through the side window

—something that smashed the front chandelier and brought instant darkness.

Already in motion when the glass globe burst into fragments, Rennevant reached the side wall just as Haggin's gun exploded, the slug ripping through the office door.

Diamond Dan yelled, "Quit it, you fool—quit firing!"

That fear-prodded command brought an amused grin to Rennevant's lips. Bannerman didn't relish the idea of being hit by a stray bullet.

A faint beam of reflected light from the hotel slanted in through the doorway, but aside from that the long room was cloaked in quilted darkness. Quickly calculating the location of the side window, Rennevant eased along the wall.

A man out front called, "What's going on in there?"

"Bring a lantern," Dan Bannerman yelled.

Someone was moving over by the bar. Haggin probably, or Sheriff Shumway. Gallego and Hallmark were keeping quiet. Those two weren't taking any chances on making targets of themselves.

Rennevant took another cautious step, and another. Then, feeling a gentle draft of rain-moistened air against his right cheek, he understood that he was in front of the window. Reaching out, he touched the sill and, tracing the opening, was strongly tempted to dive through it. But even though the move would take only a moment, it couldn't be made without some slight racket; and the jingle of a lifted spur rowel, or the scrape of a boot on the sill would be enough to betray him. The sense of probing eyes was like a creeping insect along his spine. Those waiting gunhawks couldn't see him, but if they heard him go through the window there'd be a dead deputy marshal sprawled out there in the alley.

The silence became so complete that Rennevant could hear the tiny *plop* of scattered rain drops in the alley's dust. Even the men in the street had ceased their talking, and in that hushed interval Rennevant remembered another time when strict silence had trapped him—when only a hastily devised trick had saved him. Holstering his gun, he plucked three loaded shells from the loops of his belt and, tossing them toward the room's rear corner, waited for them to land. Then, as their rattling impact set Red Haggin's gun to instant firing. Rennevant dove through the window and, landing on hands and knees, ran down the rain-drizzled alley.

Almost at once a vague shape loomed up directly ahead of him. Rennevant was snatching his gun from its holster when Piano Pete said gustily, "By God, it took you long enough to come through that window, friend Steve!"

The shooting had ceased in the saloon now, and Dan Bannerman was again calling for a lantern. Rennevant chuckled and, following Modesto into a back street, said amusedly. "So it was you smashed the chandelier."

"Yes," the old gambler admitted, stopping near the rear door of Estevan's Cafe. "It cost me a good watch to do it."

"They had me in a tight, sure enough," Rennevant said. Then he asked, "How about having a cup of coffee with me, while I finish that steak?"

"No, I guess not. Diamond Dan is going to be curious about who busted his fancy light. If we're seen together he'd guess who threw the watch, and then I'd be a gone goose."

"How about the little Mex in the cafe?" Rennevant asked. "He saw us together, and heard us talking."

Modesto said, "I'm not worrying about him. Lon

keeps his mouth shut all the time. It's a fundamental characteristic of his race, Steve."

Then he added glumly, "Cruzatte's son came home —all shot to pieces."

"Guess I heard the shooting," Rennevant reported and, recalling how a girl had screamed just before Anne Cruzatte called to her father, asked, "Has young Cruzatte got a sweetheart in town?"

Modesto nodded. "Kate Carmody, who runs the hotel she inherited from her mother. She and Bob planned to marry soon as he got enough money to put the Anvil back on its feet. He was bringing home a bankroll for that purpose."

"So that's why he was ambushed," Rennevant reflected.

Recalling Hallmark's presence at the stage road pass, he guessed that several Double D riders had been waiting for Bob Cruzatte. The pattern of this picture was beginning to take definite shape. Yet there was one part of it that still puzzled Rennevant: Piano Pete's seemingly deep interest in Cruzatte's affairs.

Modesto said worriedly, "I've got to put in an appearance at the saloon. Dan will think it's peculiar if I don't show up. He might get to wondering things."

Then he added, "Watch out for Red Haggin, Steve. He's plenty proud of his gun rep around here, and he'll make another try at you, sure as hell."

It was characteristic of Steve Rennevant that he didn't order another steak when he perched on a stool in Estevan's Cafe. Instead he had the little Mexican warm up the original meal and presently ate it with real relish. A trivial thing in itself, this eating of an interrupted steak; yet it was a symbol of the code Rennevant lived by—the stubborn code of finishing whatever he started.

And it was significant that Rennevant had chosen an end stool that allowed him to watch both the front and kitchen doorways. Bannerman's gunhawks would be on the prowl by now. They wouldn't expect to find him this close to the Border Belle, and so might miss him. But constant vigilance was also a symbol of his code.

The rain was beating down in torrents when Rennevant paid for his meal. Lon Estevan said meekly, "She is *bueno* for the cattle, thees rain. She will fill the *tenajas*."

"Yeah," Rennevant agreed, "and she may help me to reach the Cattle King without being used for a target. A galoot would sure get wet with slug holes in his clothes tonight."

Estevan's eyes widened perceptibly. "Those shooting—she was for you, senor?" he asked.

Rennevant nodded.

"You are the *amigo* of Senor Pete," the Mexican said. "*Vaya con Dios, amigo.*"

"Thanks," Rennevant said appreciatively and, walking to the door, built himself a smoke. Piano Pete, he thought, struck up strange friendships: A Mex cafe proprietor, a girl who owned a hotel, a badge-toting pariah who made enemies the way some men made money.

Glancing along the rain-swept street, Rennevant saw lamplight in front of the Border Belle. He was wondering if Modesto had gone into the saloon when the faint notes of piano music came to him—the soft, sweet strains of *Black-Eyed Susie*. Whereupon Rennevant grinned. Modesto, he guessed, was taking this way of telling him that everything was all right. Remembering how concerned the old gambler had been about getting Cruzatte out of the saloon alive, Rennevant tried to tally the real reason behind that concern. It was, he sensed, something more than the nagging of a guilty conscience, for Modesto had excused his crooked dealing on the grounds of his own survival. Yet he had been willing to risk his life to save Cruzatte from Bannerman's slaughter trap. For what reason?

"A payoff you'd never guess," the gambler had said.

Shifting his gaze to the Cattle King veranda, which was now deserted, Rennevant remembered the way Anne Cruzatte had stood there—how strongly her blond beauty had appealed to him. The thought came that she might be the reason for Piano Pete's interest. Modesto was old enough to be her father, and he didn't seem like a calico-chasing man. But Jeff Cruzatte's daughter would turn any man's head, and she might be the motive behind Modesto's secret siding of an old cattleman. What was it the French said—*cherchez la femme?*

Tilting his hat brim against the slanting rain, Rennevant went out and moved quickly away from the cafe's feeble glow of window light. It was uncommon strange that Bannerman's gunhawks hadn't discovered him in the restaurant. Surely they must have searched for him. Diamond Dan would want to settle with the man who'd made a mockery of his slick slaughter trick. And there'd been a plain look of anticipated vengeance in Sheriff Shumway's eyes a moment before the saloon light went out. Then there was Red Haggin who'd want to redeem his gunhawk reputation, and Whitey Hallmark who'd be wanting revenge for that roughing he'd taken on the stage road that afternoon. Turk Gallego hadn't seemed interested one way or the other, but Rennevant guessed that Turk's masked features never showed anything.

Where were those men now?

Why hadn't they found him?

Abruptly then the thought came to Rennevant that perhaps they *had* found him. Perhaps they were waiting along this dark street for him now!

That thought sent his hand to his holster. It halted him in midstride as he stepped into the road. But almost at once he discarded his suspicion; for he'd made a plain target a moment ago when he'd come out of the cafe. If Bannerman's bunch had been waiting he'd have known it then. Now he was no target at all.

Hock-deep mud sucked at Rennevant's boot heels as he crossed Main Street. When he reached the opposite walk he collided with a rain barrel, and thereafter held a hand in front of him until he reached the hotel steps. There he halted for a moment, peering at the Border Belle's foggy bloom of lamplight. Two or three men stood in the saloon doorway, but it was impossible to identify them through the slanting sheets of rain that screened the street. And it would be equally impossible for them to identify him.

He went up the steps and, reaching the roofed veranda, shook water from his battered hat. All this rain, he reflected, would be a godsend for the cowmen. But it would obliterate the tracks of Bob Cruzatte's attacker—and his own. Instantly then he guessed why Bannerman's slug slammers hadn't come looking for him. Knowing that Bob Cruzatte had been ambushed and that suspicion would point to Double D riders, Bannerman might have decided to use him—Rennevant—for a scapegoat!

It would be an easy thing to hang the drygulching onto an unknown saddle tramp. With all sign of the ambush washed out by this torrential downpour, there'd be no way of Rennevant proving he hadn't done the job. He was thinking about the angle when he stepped into the hotel doorway and almost collided with Sheriff Shumway.

Surprise bugged Shumway's toady eyes. "You here!" he exclaimed.

Rennevant nodded, and caught a fleeting glimpse of Jeff Cruzatte and Kate Carmody in the lobby. He gave Shumway a tough, taunting grin, and asked, "You got any objections?"

Shumway didn't answer. He kept staring at Rennevant; kept blocking the doorway with his ponderous bulk. Remembering how eager this man had been to butcher him over there in the Border Belle, Rennevant contemplated him with a narrowing regard. The sheriff, he guessed, was swayed by teetering indecision; caught between seething resentment and cowardly caution, Shumway couldn't make up his mind.

Rennevant grinned again. He reached out with his left hand, and grasped Shumway by the shirt and yanked him onto the veranda. Then, snatching the lawman's gun from its holster, he tossed it out into the mud and, deftly stepping around behind Shumway, pushed him headlong down the veranda steps.

"Don't get in my way again," Rennevant warned, and went into the hotel.

Jeff Cruzatte came forward at once, his hand outstretched. "You did me a real turn in the saloon," he declared. "I'm much obliged, and I ain't believing the hogwash Shumway just tried to shove down our throats."

Cruzatte was cold sober now. His rope-calloused fingers had a real grip in them; they reminded Rennevant of the way his father's fingers had gripped his just before the old man died. He asked, "What did Shumway try to tell you?"

"He claims it was you drygulched my son. He

said you had hightailed out of town after trying to hold up the saloon."

Rennevant said dryly, "Well, he was wrong about me leaving town—at least."

He shifted his gaze to Kate Carmody. Her black lashes were moist with recent tears; her blue eyes were studying him with an intentness that bordered on suspicion, and so he said, "I didn't see the shooting. But I heard it."

He walked over to the desk and, picking up a pen, wrote his name on the dog-eared ledger. Kate Carmody lifted a key from the rack, glanced at the ledger and said, "Number Nine, at the west end of the hall, Mister Rennevant."

Then she smiled a quick comradely smile that changed the contours of her heart-shaped face and put a twinkle into her Irish eyes. "I'm sure it wasn't you who shot Bob," she declared.

Rennevant said, "Thank you, ma'am," and was starting up the stairs when Cruzatte asked, "Would you be interested in a job? I could use a hand, if he wasn't in a hurry for payday."

"No," Rennevant said civilly. "But thanks for the offer."

He went on up the stairs and, passing an open doorway, saw Anne Cruzatte standing beside a pudgy-faced little man who sat in front of a bed. She glanced up and, coming quickly across the room, said, "Thank you for helping my father."

Her voice was low, yet it carried a rich, full urgency; and there was a glowing warmth in her eyes.

Rennevant took off his hat and for a queerly confused moment fumbled with it in silence. This tall, shapely girl possessed a quality of womanliness that strongly affected him—that made him aware of his bristly beard and soiled, rain-soaked clothing. Her oval face was tanned to a delicate gold-ivory shade that set off the lustre of her light blond hair. He wondered about the color of her eyes; if they were brown or hazel—and why her face seemed remotely familiar.

He asked finally, "How is your brother?"

"He's badly wounded," she said, and nodded toward the man at the bedside. "Doc Dineen doesn't seem to think much of Bob's chances."

Then something like stubbornness came into her voice; something that gave Rennevant a quick key to the girl's high courage. "But Bob is going to live," she declared.

"Sure," Rennevant agreed. "Sure he will."

Then, as Kate Carmody came up the stairs, he went on to his room.

Later, just as he was about to turn out the bracket lamp above his bed, Rennevant remembered the letter he had to write. Whereupon he penciled a brief note to his chief in Denver, using the page of a tally-book.

"The Faro Kid beat me to the Border," he wrote. "But I may be able to corral the Whitey Hallmark gang. If they are still wanted, send me warrants and full descriptions. Will await your instructions."

4

AWAKE early, Rennevant was out of his room before sunup. Bob Cruzatte's door was closed, and the lobby was deserted when he went downstairs. The rain had ceased sometime during the night and the sky was clear, but Main Street's muddy pools gave graphic proof of the storm's intensity.

Standing at the top of the veranda steps, Rennevant sent a roving glance along the street. San Sabino
looked different in daylight; the town looked peaceful and commonplace and a trifle shabby. A negro
swamper was washing cuspidors in a large wooden
bucket on the Border Belle stoop; farther along the
street a man in a derby hat was unlocking the barbershop door, and down at the livery Hook Hooligan
led two horses to the watering trough.

Except for that Main Street showed no signs of
life. But beyond, where pepper trees lined a back
street, thin tendrils of wood smoke spiraled from
chimneys and two women gossiped over a sagging
picket fence.

One woman said, "Such goings on! Shooting and
robbing and what not!"

Her companion complained, "It's no fit place for
a body to live any more. Seems like Mayor Matabelle
could do something about it!"

Rennevant picked his way across the muddy
street and, going to the post office, mailed his letter.
Then he had breakfast at Estevan's Cafe and afterward sauntered down to the livery and watched
Hooligan water horses.

When the old Irishman brought Rowdy out, the
sorrel stepped gimpily, as if sore in front. "Yer hoss
acts like he's goin' lame," Hooligan muttered. "Ye
must of rid hell out of him yestiddy."

Rowdy nickered, and nuzzled Rennevant's vest
pocket for the licorice drop he invariably received
each morning. But because Rennevant had a sudden,
startling hunch, he ignored the sorrel's teasing. He
lifted a front foot and, examining the frog, found
what he'd suspected he would find—a horseshoe nail
driven full length into the tender nerve center of
the hoof!

"Damnation!" Hooligan exclaimed, and when Rennevant lifted the other foot, Hook blurted: "Maimed in both feet!"

Rennevant's voice was low when he finally spoke; low and cold and sharp as wind-driven sleet. "Was Whitey Hallmark around your barn late last night?" he demanded.

"Yes, he saddled up his own bronc late—after I'd turned in," Hook reported.

"The dirty son!" Rennevant muttered. "The dirty, stinking son!"

Then, while Hook pulled the nails with pliers, he fed Rowdy a licorice drop and cursed savagely as blood spurted from each nail hole. It didn't seem possible a man could be so downright low as to take out his spite on an innocent horse—not even a killer renegade like Whitey Hallmark.

"I'll doctor him for ye," Hook said, "but he'll be laid up for a spell."

Swabbing the wounds with disinfectant he asked wonderingly, "Why would Hallmark do that?"

"Because I slapped his homely face out on the road yesterday," Rennevant said.

"Ye slapped Whitey Hallmark's face?" Hook blurted unbelievingly.

Rennevant nodded, whereat Hook eyed him in amazement. "Whitey is supposed to be high-heeled hell with a gun—almost as fast as Red Haggin!"

Afterward, when the sorrel had been made comfortable in a well-bedded stall, the liveryman said, "Jules Larson told me you saved Cruzatte's bacon in the Border Belle last night. I was mistook about ye, lad, and I shouldn't of been so short with me answers. Is there anythin' else ye'd be wantin' to know about this town?"

There were several things Rennevant wanted to know, but he doubted if this monkey-faced old Irishman could give him the answers.

He asked. "Do you happen to know where Pete Modesto lives?"

"At the Cattle King," Hooligan reported. "He's a funny jigger, that one. He makes his livin' with gamblin' cards, but he'd rather play the pianer than eat. He's been givin' music lessons to Kate Carmody, and there's them that thinks he's more than a trifle sweet on the girl. But if he is—and mind ye, I'm not the one who says so—he's awastin' of his time, for Kate worships the ground young Bob walks on."

This *was* information. But it didn't solve any part of the puzzle for Rennevant. In fact, it made the whole deal more complicated. If Piano Pete had a case on Kate Carmody, why should he be so solicitous of the Cruzattes' welfare?

Then Hooligan said something that set Rennevant to thinking along an entirely different angle. The liveryman said, "Pete's also been givin' music lessons to a homesteader's kids over on Mesquite Flats."

"Did he give one yesterday afternoon?" Rennevant asked.

Hooligan thought for a moment, then nodded. "Pete rode in just ahead of Whitey Hallmark," he said.

Remembering that Modesto had mentioned the fact that Gallego and Haggin had also ridden into town about sundown, Rennevant said, "Seems like everybody and his brother was riding around this country yesterday afternoon."

Thereupon he sauntered over to the barbershop and, ordering a shave, lay back in the chair with a sigh. Last night he'd suspected that either Red Haggin or Turk Gallego had shot Bob Cruzatte. Now, because five years in the law game had taught him the folly of playing favorites, he had to include Piano Pete in the list of suspects. It seemed almost inconceivable that Modesto could have done so vicious a chore. Yet many a peaceable man had gone temporarily berserk because of a girl's smiling lips. And if Modesto "had a case" on Kate Carmody there'd be a motive for his attack on Bob Cruzatte.

While the barber lathered his face, Rennevant put his mind to a methodical examination of facts and faces and half-formed impressions. But when the shave was ended, he had found no plausible explanation of the riddle. That half-filled canteen, and his regard for Rowdy's comfort, had sure started something up there on Cascabelle Divide yesterday. Something that might take a lot of finishing.

Stepping out from the barbershop, Rennevant saw Jeff Cruzatte climb into a red-wheeled rig at the livery. The old cowman waved to Anne, who stood on the hotel veranda, then drove west on Main Street. A shining black buggy stopped in front of Matabelle's Mercantile. One of its two occupants alighted: a tall, fashionably garbed man with a Michaelmas daisy in his lapel.

Rennevant glanced at the barber, who was standing behind him in the doorway, and asked: "Who's the tall dude?"

"John Matabelle," the barber reported. "Mayor, merchant and Number One resident of Society Hill."

The other man, also well-dressed, but shorter and more slightly built than Matabelle, drove past the barbershop and tooled the rig up in front of the livery.

"That's Tate Kiley," the barber offered. "He's president of the San Sabino Bank, and Number Two man on the Hill. Him and Matabelle used to have the big say in this town until Dan Bannerman came in and sort of cramped their style."

"So?" Rennevant mused, and noticed that the barber was eyeing him with sudden interest.

"Say—ain't you the pilgrim that shot up the saloon last night?" the barber demanded.

Rennevant grinned and shook his head. "Haven't fired a gun in almost a month," he said truthfully, and went on along the street.

Anne Cruzatte was still standing on the hotel veranda, waching her father drive out of town. She started to turn toward the doorway, then stopped abruptly. For a full moment, while Rennevant sauntered forward, she stood gazing at something or someone across the street.

Rennevant was wondering about that when she called, "Good morning, Mister Haggin!"

The significance of those words struck Rennevant instantly. They must mean that Red Haggin was waiting in the alley just beyond the bank—that Anne was taking this method of exposing the gunhawk's presence!

Stepping quickly out into the road, Rennevant crossed the street at an angle which allowed him to keep a constant watch on the alley head. He had gained the opposite sidewalk when Haggin stepped up to the Border Belle stoop and stood just west of the doorway, a squatty, roan-faced man with a broken nose and protruding teeth. Seeing him now for the first time, Rennevant felt a familiar thrust of anticipation. Here was another tough hombre all cocked for trouble; another impatient slug slammer who needed honing down to size.

Anne Cruzatte remained motionless on the Cattle King veranda. She watched Rennevant closely, smiling a little at the picture he made. He looked younger now, with the stubby whiskers shaved from his face. A devil-be-damned grin quirked his long lips, giving him a youthful, almost boyish expression. But there was nothing youthful in the tight wariness of his smoky eyes, nor in the way he held his head as he tromped the sunlit planks. He looked like a lean lobo on the prowl.

Rennevant was almost to the hotel now; near enough for Anne to see the crinkly lines at the corners of his sun-puckered eyes, and the way his gun swayed gently to his leisurely stride. Wary, tight-eyed drifters were no novelty in San Sabino, but this tall stranger was different. Just how, she couldn't say, unless it was because of his boyish grin and the whimsical, almost hungry way he'd looked at her last night.

Rennevant called quietly, "You looking for somebody, Haggin?"

The redhead didn't answer at once. He gazed at Rennevant for a full moment, as if by this prolonged scrutiny he could calculate the speed and accuracy of Rennevant's right hand. Then he said, "I might be lookin' for a smart-alecky galoot about your size."

His voice had a nasal, high-pitched twang to it. Yet it held a tone of absolute confidence and the brashness of a man accustomed to having his way.

Rennevant's grin grew broader, "Mebbe," he taunted, "you need glasses, Red."

He was within ten feet of the hotel now. Another few steps would put him directly opposite Haggin. Not shifting his gaze, he said to Anne, "You better go inside, ma'am."

Stepping quickly to the lobby's front window, she watched Rennevant reach the corner of the building. There he stopped and stood facing Haggin across thirty feet of sunlit dust. A rash, mocking smile slanted his lean cheeks, and he said flatly, "You're no ornament to this street, Red. Grab—or git!"

Rennevant's blunt command seemed to startle Red Haggin. It seemed to drive a wedge of indecision into him. Remembering how he had bullied other men, Anne watched him closely and felt a surge of satisfaction. Steve Rennevant was ramming Red's reputation down his throat—was deliberately inviting him to fight!

Turk Gallego came through the batwings and stood just clear of them, peering briefly at Rennevant. He said something to Haggin, speaking so softly that the words didn't carry across the street. Then he went back into the saloon.

Rennevant kept watching Haggin; kept waiting for him to make up his mind. He asked finally, "Well, what's it going to be?"

The fingers of Haggin's right hand eased an inch closer to his gun. Anne thought: Now he's going to grab, and he's awfully fast!

Doc Dineen came downstairs. "That brother of yours is too tough to die," the medico reported. "He just smiled at Kate."

"Swell!" Anne exclaimed and, motioning for Dineen to join her, said warningly, "Don't go out just now, Doc. I expect there may be some shooting."

Rennevant took out his Durham sack, using his left hand for this chore. When he lifted the tobacco sack to his teeth and pulled it open, Doc Dineen exclaimed, "The darn crazy fool is fixing to roll a cigarette!"

Anne didn't speak, and for a moment, she didn't breathe. She just stood there watching Red Haggin's right hand—expecting to see it flash up with a blasting gun. For a seemingly endless interval while Haggin stood like a crouched statue, the street became so quiet that Anne could hear the murmur of voices in Bob's room upstairs. Someone came along the hall, started down the stairs. . . .

Then Rennevant called proddingly, "Come on, come on. Play or pass!"

Red Haggin passed. He sidestepped to the batwings and basked through them like a clown leaving a stage. Whereupon Anne sighed and smiled and, turning toward the stairway, saw Pete Modesto, looking pale and sick as he always looked in the morning. The old gambler went out and crossed the street, scarcely noticing Rennevant. Down at the livery stable Hooligan slapped his knee with the steel hook and, wincing at the impact, blurted, "The redhead turned tail, bejasus!"

A few doors up the street a mystified barber stood goggle-eyed; over in the Mercantile doorway Mayor Matabelle loosed a gasp of utter astonishment, and Jules Larson exclaimed, "There's the man we need, John—a professional gunman!"

Doc Dineen came out of the hotel and peered over his glasses at Rennevant. "That was Kettledrum Basin's bad boy you were talking to," he said. "Nobody ever talked to Red like that before."

Rennevant chuckled and, going into the hotel, found Anne waiting in the lobby.

She said smilingly, "You play rough, don't you, Steve Rennevant?"

Again, as on the previous night, confusion disrupted the orderly run of Rennevant's thoughts. But he managed to ask, "How's your brother this morning?"

"Bob is going to live," she declared happily. "Even Doc Dineen agrees with me now!"

Then she said, "Dad tells me you turned down his offer of a job last night."

"Yes," Rennevant acknowledged, and decided that her eyes were dark hazel, and that they were the most beautiful—the most expressive eyes he'd ever seen. And that they had the longest, blackest lashes . . .

She asked, "Wouldn't your plans permit you to

ride for Dad, until my brother gets well enough to ride?"

"Well, not exactly," Rennevant said. "I'm sorry for your father, being so short-handed and all. But—well, you see, ma'am, my gun isn't for hire."

"I know you're not a professional gunhawk," she said quickly.

"How would you know that?" Rennevant asked, and saw embarrassment put a rose stain in her cheeks.

"I—I sensed it last night, when you stood in the hall," she said in a hushed, confessional voice. "I don't know what you are, Steve Rennevant—but you're no hired killer. I'm sure of that."

Something in the words, and the way she said them, put a high flare of satisfaction in Rennevant. For upwards of five years men had called him a merciless killer—a tin-star killer without mercy or tolerance. They'd given his gun skill grudging respect, but they'd shunned him as a man apart from other men. Yet this warm-eyed girl was saying she knew he was something more than a grisly pariah!

And she was plucking at his sleeve, saying softly, urgently, "Won't you give us a hand, for just a little while? We've got so much work to do, and so little time to do it. Unless Bannerman's cattle are driven off our grass, we'll have no winter graze left at all."

Even then, with the feel of her fingers on his arm stirring his pulse to a faster rhythm, Rennevant had no intention of granting her request. Hell, a man couldn't let a girl's soft words and glowing eyes interfere with duty—even though she'd saved him from Haggin's sneak play a few minutes before. Then abruptly it occurred to him that he wouldn't be leaving this country for at least two weeks—perhaps longer. If he remained here without working, someone might suspect he was a badgetoter, and spoil his chance of corraling the Hallmark gang.

Anne spoke again, still in that low, confessing tone. "I never was really afraid in my life, until last night when Dad went into the Border Belle," she said. "I'd never known what fear was like. But I know now."

Rennevant fingered his sweat-stained hat. He kept seeing all the things in Anne he'd ever dreamed of seeing in a girl. And because he knew that a man-hunting lawdog had no right to romantic notions, he damned himself for seeing them. But it was no use. Even if he'd shut his eyes—if he'd turned away and ridden a thousand miles—he'd still have seen her.

"All right," he said finally. "I'll ride for your father, just as a cowhand, and not as a gun rider. And I'm only staying a couple of weeks. Please remember that, ma'am."

A quick smile curved her fulsome lips. She reached out and took his hand and said, "I will. I'll remember our bargain, Steve. And from now on don't call me ma'am. My name is Anne."

The intimate tone of her voice and the pressure of her slim fingers affected him tremendously. They put an emotion in him different from anything he'd ever felt. It was like hunger, or thirst; yet it had urgent impulses and the buoyancy of high exaltation mixed with it. Rennevant had ceased being surprised at Fate's frivolous tricks, and so he accepted this one with sardonic amusement. A man's destiny followed devious designs; a man had little to do with the weaving of its strands, nor with the ultimate shaping of its pattern.

"All right, Anne," he said softly.

For a brief moment then, while they stood with eyes in close communion, Steve Rennevant understood why countless men had fought and toiled and died for the women of their choice. Remembering that Dan Bannerman had endeavored to win this girl, he understood Diamond Dan's insistent desire to possess her. Here was completeness for a man; here was warmth and beauty and fragrance—a living shrine to worship and sustain.

And because all his perceptions were keyed to this fleeting, flawless clarity, Rennevant sensed a kindred emotion in Anne; knew without question that she shared some portion of the rising flame inside him. As if in frank admission of that fact, her fingers tugged gently for release and she said, "Please, Steve."

Her voice was low, little more than a whisper. But the throb of suppressed excitement in it showed how surely she shared the emotion she'd aroused in him —how high a flame they had kindled together.

He released her fingers, and when she said, "It's cooler outside," he went with her to the tree-shaded bench at the far end of the veranda.

Presently he asked, "Why is Bannerman so set on owning the Anvil?"

"Because he's a born range hog," Anne said. "The Anvil and the Homestead Hills would give the Double D a clean sweep to the Mexican Border. If Bannerman owned the Anvil he'd crowd the small outfits from the Homestead Hills without bothering to buy them, and he'd have enough graze to run the biggest bunch of cattle in Arizona Territory."

"Well," Rennevant drawled, "it's not a new idea. According to the Bible, they had range-grabbing trouble way back when the Israelites were running cattle on the mesa land east of Jerusalem. I don't know whether those old-timey cowpokes used center-fire saddles or double rigs, but they had the same ideas about grass and water."

Anne eyed him wonderingly, "I would never have guessed you were a Bible reader," she said.

"I'm not. But my father was a religious man."

An old bitterness edged his voice when he added, "My father believed in the Bible, and came as close to following it as a cowman could, but he died cussing the thieves that shot him."

Watching him closely as he spoke, Anne saw how his eyes changed; how hard and cold they got. In the space of a few seconds every bit of warmth went out of them. She asked, "Is that why you take pleasure in fighting men like Red Haggin—because you don't like thieves?"

"I hate them," Rennevant said flatly.

5

Mayor Matabelle came across the veranda and spoke to Anne. Rennevant was making ready to leave, when the mayor asked, "Are you going to ride for the Anvil?"

Rennevant nodded, giving the old merchant a deliberate appraisal.

"Then I want you to hear what I've got to say," Matabelle declared, and joined them on the bench. "I've tried to stay clear of range squabbles," he said in a hushed, yet excited voice. "But it looks like we'll never have any peace around here until Dan Bannerman is chipped down to size. He's trying to talk Tate Kiley into foreclosing mortgages on five Pool ranches, and he wants Tate to sell them to him at half their real value. Tate doesn't want to do it, but the bank is over-loaned and can't finance a holdout fight against the Double D."

"What," Anne inquired, "has that to do with us? Dad tried to tell Larson's bunch six months ago what would happen. But they wouldn't help him buck Bannerman."

Matabelle sighed wearily. "I know—I know," he muttered. "We all thought Jeff was just stirring up trouble for no good reason. We didn't believe Bannerman would try to hog the whole Basin. I don't like to see range war come—but I'm not going to sit idly by and let Bannerman get control of our bank, and everything else in this town. So I've decided to back the Pool with whatever money is needed to fight him to a finish, no matter how long it takes. Jules Larson says his members will all swing into line with your father—if Rennevant will rod the fight against the Double D."

A quick smile curved Anne's lips. But Rennevant didn't smile. He asked moodily, "Why do they want me in on the deal?"

"Because you stood off Bannerman's toughs in the saloon last night, and bluffed Red Haggin into quitting like a yellow dog this morning," Matabelle explained.

He glanced at Rennevant's tied-down holster and said, "They want one gunslick on their side—somebody who knows the tricks of the trade."

A cynical grin twisted Rennevant's lips. Here it was again; the same old grudging respect for his skill with a gun—for a grisly pariah *who knew the tricks of the trade.* This peace-loving old merchant would never guess the price a man paid to learn those tricks; he wouldn't know how lonesome a drifting gunslinger could get, nor how many times the cold fingers of fear clawed at a man's inwards when the odds stacked up.

Recalling how Jeff Cruzatte had refused Larson's advice in the saloon the night before, Rennevant turned to Anne and said, "Your father told Larson he wanted no truck with the Pool bunch at all."

"But this is different," Anne exclaimed. "This is a chance to save the Anvil!"

Matabelle asked, "Will you run the show, Rennevant?"

Which was a question Steve Rennevant didn't like to answer. Siding a bankrupt old cowman for a couple of weeks was one thing. Leading an organization in a bloody range war was something quite different; something a deputy marshal had no right to do. Finally he said, "Reckon I'd better talk it over with Mister Cruzatte first. It's his fight—not mine."

Whereupon Anne declared, "We'll drive out to the Anvil right now. I can hardly wait to tell Dad the news."

Afterward, when she had rented a rig at Hooligan's Livery and Rennevant had stowed his riding gear in back, Anne drove out of San Sabino at a fast trot, feeling happier than she'd felt in months.

"I'm sure Dad will join the Pool," she said. "He's called them a cowardly, no-good bunch time and again, but that was because they wouldn't fight."

"So," Rennevant mused, eyeing the country ahead with a drifter's strict attention for landmarks.

Watching him, Anne tried to guess his age. Right now, with a sober straightness to his lips and his sun-puckered eyes questing the slopes of Sashay Ridge, he had the mature look of a man who'd wandered a long time in many places. Yet when he grinned he looked no older than Bob, who was twenty-four.

She said softly, "A *centavo* for your thoughts," and watched a slow grin change the planes of his face.

"Not worth it," he said, digging out his Durham sack. Then, as his fingers shaped up a cigarette with practiced skill, he told her about Rowdy.

Even though he spoke no definite word of affection for his horse, the controlled emotion in his voice showed how close a comradeship there'd been between them. Which was another link in Anne's forming chain of impressions. He loved horses, he had voiced a deep-rooted hatred for thieves, and he had risked his life to save her father from almost certain death the night before. It all added up to confirm her first hasty, half-formed impression—that despite his toughness and his skill with guns, this wary-eyed rider was thoroughly honest. And perhaps a trifle lonely.

"I'll pay Hallmark for taking his spite out on Rowdy," Rennevant said, "and I'll do it with my fists. Shooting is too good for that kind of snake."

"Shooting," Anne said cynically, "is too good for most of the Double D bunch. They'd have been hung long ago if law badges were worth the tin they're made of."

Rennevant asked slyly, "You don't think much of badgetoters, do you, Anne?"

"I do not!" she said emphatically.

Rennevant grinned, and for a time, while the rig clattered up the long, rocky slope of Sashay Ridge, they rode in silence. He covertly studied Anne's profile at intervals, knowing that she was the most beautiful girl he'd ever seen and wanting to have a permanent picture of her in his mind—something to remember on lonely nights.

At the crest of the ridge Anne halted the horse for a brief rest, and Rennevant asked, "Just what does Matabelle stand to win by backing the fight against the Double D?"

"Nothing, except that beating Bannerman would make San Sabino a decent town to live in," Anne explained.

"Never knew a politician who wasn't trying to get something for himself," Rennevant said. "Money or power or glory. They're a sorry breed, mostly, and out for what they can get."

Anne laughed. "But you don't know John Matabelle. He's been mayor so long he looks on San Sabino as his personal property, and he doesn't want it to get a bad reputation in the Territory."

Rennevant shrugged. "Well, I don't like to get mixed up in a range war." He was searching for words to explain his reluctance when Anne's fingers gripped his arm.

"I wish you would," she said urgently.

The feel of those slim fingers roused a richer awareness of her presence—made him sense again how surely she shared the strong run of emotion he felt. Her face was turned toward him now so that he could see the full sweet curve of her lips; they parted slightly as he watched, and she whispered, "I wish you would, Steve."

Something flared up in Rennevant then; something he couldn't control. He said, "All right," and, putting his arms around her, added rashly, "There's something else I'd like to do."

"I—I wish you would," Anne whispered again, and was gently smiling when he kissed her.

For a timeless interval their lips met and merged and sheer ecstasy had its way with Steve Rennevant. It was as if this girl had always belonged to him; as if she'd never been a stranger. Here was completeness beyond compare, for her lips were giving him more than surrender; they were answering gladly, generously, with all the wild sweet flavor of a girl in love. And because she was so close and yielding against him, the beating of her heart was like his own heart beating.

Presently Anne murmured, "Please," and he released her. She took a moment to rearrange her tumbled hair, and in that brief interval of silence they both heard the thudding tromp of a hard-ridden horse behind them. . . .

Jules Larson strode out of Matabelle's Mercantile with a broad smile on his angular, weather-beaten face. "I'll back your Pool to the limit," the mayor had just told him, "and I believe you'll have Steve Rennevant for a gun boss."

That meant the waiting was over. It meant an end to the women's talk of patience; of hungry kids and empty guns. No more shameful sidestepping when Bannerman's brazen riders pushed Double D steers through the Homestead Hills; no more coward-calling by Jeff Cruzatte. With Matabelle furnishing food for their families and ammunition for their guns, every member of the Pool would fight—gladly. And with a topnotch gunman like Rennevant to lead them, they'd win.

Hurriedly, in the fashion of a man with important news, Larson went down Border Belle Alley to the blacksmith shop where Alex Engle was having a buckboard repaired. "Matabelle backs us to the limit," he told the young cowman. "Anne Cruzatte just left for the Anvil, and Steve Rennevant went with her."

"Good!" Engle exclaimed, a rash smile dimpling his round, boyish face. "I'll pass the word to Jim Highbaugh and Luke Yancey on my way home. You tell the others."

Larson nodded, and said, "The waiting is done, Alex. Now we fight!"

He went back up the alley and was passing the open doorway at the rear of the Border Belle Saloon when he heard Dan Bannerman's angry voice. "Swear in Red and Turk as deputies," the big man bellowed. "And arrest Rennevant before he reaches the Anvil."

Then Sheriff Shumway's voice asking, "What charge will I arrest him on?"

"Robbery, rustling—anything. Only be goddam sure he gets killed resisting arrest!"

The sheriff spoke again, but Larson didn't wait to hear any more. Turning abruptly through the Wells Fargo wagon yard, he ran to Hooligan's stable, saddled his horse and rode out of town. And because Steve Rennevant's death now would be a tragic blow to the Pool's chances for victory, he urged the bronc to a hard run.

For a time, while Larson galloped through the greasewood breaks west of San Sabino, he failed to sight the livery rig. Glancing back at frequent intervals and seeing no sign of riders behind him, he felt a growing optimism. There might be a chance for the rig to race to Anvil ahead of the posse if he warned Rennevant in time.

But when he glanced back again, his hope died instantly. A plume of dust was boiling above three riders on the road just out of town; and a moment later, as Larson crossed a secondary ridge, he saw the livery rig topping the summit ahead of him. That meant there wouldn't be a chance for the rig to outrun the posse. Not a glimmer of a chance!

Spurring his horse up Sashay Ridge, Larson overtook the buggy and blurted out his warning. When Rennevant showed no sign of apprehension, he added nervously, "They're coming fast!"

"So," Rennevant mused, and glanced speculatively at Larson's rat-tailed roan. Then he said, "I hear you want me to ramrod the fight against the Double D."

"We do," Larson exclaimed. "We are depending on it."

"Then I'll start right now, by borrowing your bronc," Rennevant said, getting down from the rig. "I'll use my own saddle."

Larson said, "Sure," and hastily stripped his gear from the panting bronc.

"What are you planning to do, Steve?" Anne asked.

Rennevant grinned—a reckless, boyish grin that reminded her of Bob.

"I'm going back and meet Bannerman's posse," he said, lifting his saddle from the rear of the rig.

Watching him, Anne thought she knew why he was a drifter. He had a fighter's relish for conflict; it showed in his grin, and in the way his eyes turned smoky blue at time like this. Yet he hadn't wanted to get mixed up in a range war, and that seemed strange. In fact it seemed downright puzzling to Anne. . . .

Rennevant climbed into saddle and, drawing a Winchester from its scabbard, said, "I've got something here that'll slow those three dudes down a bit —while you folks drive to the ranch."

Then he asked, "Just where is the Anvil from here?"

Anne pointed west, toward the Rampart Mountains, and said, "Use that high chimney peak for a marker, Steve. Anvil is three miles due east of it. This is Sashay Ridge. It angles northward into the Homestead Hills, which separates Anvil and Double D range."

"Just like handing me a map," Rennevant drawled, and rode back across the ridge.

Anne called, "Good luck, Steve."

"Thanks," he said, and just before he rode over the rim, added grinningly, "See you at supper time, Anne."

Jules Larson rubbed his sweat-stained face. "A born gunman, that Rennevant," he declared. "No normal feelin's at all!"

Remembering Steve's ardent embrace, and the

hungry way he'd kissed her a few moments ago, Anne smiled secretively. "He's a first-class fighting man," she murmured, "but he has feelings, too—real feelings."

Which was something for Jules Larson to puzzle out as he drove the livery rig toward the Anvil.

Riding a little distance down the east slope of the ridge, Rennevant eased the roan out onto a projecting ledge and had his look at the country beyond. Nothing showed in the greasewood breaks, and for a brief interval he failed to distinguish sign of movement on the tilted, hairpin turns of the road. But presently a thin dust drifted above a hidden switchback, and a moment later three riders appeared, coming up the road at a trot.

Sun glare reflected sharply on Shumway's law badge; it put a shine on Turk Gallego's dark, perspiring face and brightened the ruddy stubble of whiskers on Red Haggin's heavy cheeks. They were less than half a mile away, their sweat-lathered broncs showing how fast they'd made the run from San Sabino. Giving their gear a prolonged study, Rennevant decided that Gallego and Haggin both had rifles in saddle scabbards. He couldn't be sure about the sheriff.

And at that moment Haggin peered up at him, halted instantly and snatched out his saddle gun. Whereupon Rennevant fired.

That first shot spooked Larson's bronc into a tantrum. It also sent those three riders scampering for cover on both sides of the road. Rennevant took time to quiet the roan; he heard Sheriff Shumway yell: "It's Rennevant!" and heard the nearby sizzle of a slug before the rifle's report drifted up to him. He spotted Shumway and tried to target the dodging sheriff with two shots, but the fiddle-footed roan made accurate shooting impossible. One of those guns below was sending slugs too close for comfort. A bullet whanged within inches of his head; another spattered off a boulder less than a yard away. It was time to move.

Whirling the roan, Rennevant headed northward along the ledge, purposely remaining in sight so that the men below could see the direction of his departure. Red Haggin had dismounted and was taking time for deliberate aim; Gallego was rushing his horse along the slope, evidently intending to cut him off from town. And Sheriff Shumway was now riding up the road to come in behind him.

Whereupon Rennevant grinned and urged his horse to a faster pace. They were a crafty trio, those three—wise in the ways of backtrail fighting. But he knew a few tricks himself, even though this was the first time he'd ever been on the dodging end of a chase.

Angling up to the summit, Rennevant went northward. This, he decided, was a good chance to have a look at the Homestead Hills, and if the Double D crew were pushing cattle onto Anvil range again today, he might meet up with Whitey Hallmark. Remembering how blood had spurted from Rowdy's front feet that morning, Rennevant felt the same shocked anger he'd felt at Hooligan's stable, and a familiar, itching urge for vengeance.

Presently quartering into a trail, Rennevant followed it into a deep canyon that notched the ridge. The runoff from last night's rain had formed a sizeable creek at which he watered the roan and took a drink himself. Then, listening for the sound of pursuit and hearing the remote rumor of running horses, he splashed downstream for nearly three miles, until he found a pool where a bunch of range broncs had recently drunk. Here he turned north again, the roan's hoofprints merging with a jumble of fresh tracks that pocked the muddy bank.

"Only an Injun could track us out of here," Rennevant mused and, crossing the canyon, headed up-ridge at an angle that brought him back into the summit trail at noon.

The ridge here was covered with live oak and thickets of manzanita. Climbing a high outcrop of rock, Rennevant scouted his backtrail, seeing no sign of the three-man posse. Eastward the land dropped down to brush-blotched flats that ran all the way back to the base of Cascabelle Divide. West of him Anvil Range was a hazy sprawl of long mesas and wide valleys stretching west to the Ramparts and north to the timbered slopes of the Homestead Hills.

Squinting his eyes against the sun's harsh glare, Rennevant tallied the chimney peak Anne had pointed out, then scanned the country east of it until he picked up the far-off flash of a sun-glinted windmill. The distance was too great for him to distinguish more than a vague outline of buildings and corrals; but this remote view gave him a chance to chart Anvil's exact relation to other landmarks so that he'd have no trouble reaching it.

He was debating the advisability of riding that way now, when he noticed a high haze of dust to the northeast. The wooded hills hid whatever was below the dust, but the thought came to Rennevant that it might be another drive of Double D steers toward the Anvil. If it was, Whitey Hallmark would be bossing it. So thinking, Rennevant put his mount to a swift run.

The trail dipped occasionally, winding through ravines and crossing dry washes, but mostly its course was northward, toward the continuing dust haze. Within three miles the manzanita and oak gave way to parade-like ranks of wind-twisted pine, and

soon after that Rennevant halted on a timbered hill
directly above a homestead clearing. Upwards of
two hundred steers were being driven through the
clearing by five riders, the cattle passing between
a new log house and a pole corral.

This, then, was the way Bannerman was planning
to force Jeff Cruzatte off the Anvil—by crowding
Anvil graze, devastating what little grass remained
after the recently ended drought. And because the
Pool members had refused to fight, the Double D
used their range for a cattle trail to Anvil. . . .

Eagerly, like a lobo questing for quarry, Rennevant studied the faces of the dust-hazed riders below
him, seeking Whitey Hallmark—not finding him as
the herd tromped by the homestead and passed on
into the timber. Then a shrill voice drifted up from
the house and, glancing that way, he saw Hallmark
grappling with a gingham-clad girl!

Rennevant went down the wooded slope at a run.
Pine needles here made a thick carpet that muffled
the bronc's hoofbeats, and because Hallmark's attention was completely centered on the struggling, sobbing girl, he failed to see Rennevant dismount beside
the house.

"A few kisses won't kill you," Hallmark was saying
insistently.

He forced the girl back against the door frame
hard enough to tumble her high-coiled hair into loose
disorder. He held her so she couldn't dodge his
passion-pouted lips. But the kiss was brief.

Rennevant grasped Hallmark's shoulder, jerked
him around and bashed his nose with a short-arcing
jab. Then, as Hallmark cursed and grabbed for his
gun, Rennevant hit him hard on the chin.

The Double D foreman forgot about his gun. He
staggered back in loose-jointed confusion. He ducked

Rennevant's next swing and took a teetering step sideways, like a drunkard at a dance.

"Fight—you lady-chasin' dude!" Rennevant growled contemptuously.

His hate was a flame inside him—a high, hot flame that turned him savage. He rushed Hallmark with both fists, battered down the whitehead's guarding arms and smashed him in the face. Hallmark's knees sagged and he started to go down, but Rennevant reached out and grasped the front of Hallmark's shirt. He punched him in the stomach, propped him up and punched his slack-lipped mouth. Then, deliberately measuring Hallmark's bloody, blank-eyed face, Rennevant hit him with a long-looping right flush to the jaw. Whereupon Whitey went down—and out.

For a moment the silence was broken only by the girl's soft sobbing. She was small and dark-haired, with a graphic, girlish beauty. She stared at Hallmark's motionless form as if still fearing him. Then she glanced at Rennevant and said, "He did the same thing last week. I didn't tell my husband, because I was afraid to have him fight a gunslick killer. But I'll tell him now."

Rennevant wiped his bloody knuckles on his pants. He stooped down, unbuckled Hallmark's gun gear and handed it to the girl. "A gun and bullets make good companions when you're alone," he said quietly.

The girl was trembling, so near physical exhaustion that the holstered gun and belt seemed almost too heavy for her to hold. She said, "Thanks for your help," and smiled up at him through tear-misted eyes. "Thanks a lot."

"Who is your husband?" Rennevant inquired.

"Alex Engle. He's in town with my father—Jules Larson."

Rennevant chuckled. Fate, he reflected, was still

playing tricks. He said, "You don't owe me any thanks, ma'am. Your father's warning probably saved my life a couple of hours ago. That makes us all even."

"How strange," Mrs. Engle exclaimed, then added reverently, "Providence must have had a hand in it."

"Mebbeso," Rennevant mused and, glancing at Hallmark, saw that his boots were moving.

Those boots, he noticed, were brand new; so new their soles were scarcely marked at all. New, high-heeled boots with fancy stitching and stiff, unscuffed soles . . .

A kind of brutal anticipation took hold of Rennevant as he watched the Double D ramrod regain consciousness. It replaced the urgent need for conflict in him—the need Hallmark had cheated by refusing to fight.

Turning to Mrs. Engle, he said, "You'd better go into the house, and stay there until your husband returns, ma'am. And if any Double D riders come asking about Whitey, just tell them he rode off with a galoot named Steve Rennevant. That should give them something to think about."

Then, as Hallmark got slowly to his feet, Rennevant walked over to him and said savagely, "Fork your bronc, Romeo. We're taking a little *pasear*."

"Where we goin'?"

"To the Double D," Rennevant muttered, "or in that general direction."

Then he shoved Hallmark toward his bronc.

6

Two MILES northwest of Engle's homestead, Rennevant called an order to Hallmark who rode directly ahead of him: "Get down."

There were on a rock-studded strip of table land hemmed in on all sides by rearing, wooded hills and far enough from the cattle trail so there'd be no likelihood of meeting Double D riders. It suited Rennevant's purpose perfectly. . . .

Hallmark's bashed nose was still bleeding. He kept wiping it on his sleeve, smearing blood across his swollen jaw. "What you aimin' to do?" he demanded thickly through puffed, broken lips.

Rennevant ignored the question. He said, "Turn around," and when Whitey hesitated, knocked him around with a jolt that made Hallmark grunt.

"I didn't do nothin' but kiss her," Hallmark whined. "I wasn't plannin' her no harm—honest I wasn't."

"You got paid off for that at the homestead," Rennevant said, tying Hallmark's hands securely behind him. "This is for something else, Whitey. This is to show you how a horse feels with two nail-punctured feet."

That silenced the Double D foreman, bringing no denial. But when Rennevant unbridled Hallmark's horse and shooed it off with a slap on the rump, the scar-faced rider blurted, "It's eighteen miles to the Double D!"

"Yeah," Rennevant grunted and, getting into saddle, slacked out a few feet of rope.

"You figgerin' to make me walk it?" Hallmark demanded.

"Yeah," Rennevant said. "Every goddam step of it. Move on!"

"But I'm wearin' new boots," Whitey complained. "This is the first time I've wore 'em."

"So I noticed," Rennevant acknowledged. "After a few miles they'll feel like they're lined with sandpaper. Go on—get going."

And when Hallmark stubbornly refused to move Rennevant touched spurs to his mount. The roan lunged forward, the rope snapped taut, and Whitey Hallmark yelped. But he didn't go down. He ran behind the roan like a well-broken pack horse.

That was the way it started, that strange *pasear* toward the Double D. And although Rennevant soon pulled the bronc down to a walk, there was no stopping for rests, nor for water at occasional gullies, nor for a looksee on the many ridges they topped. Steadily, and silently, except for the one time he inquired the direction to the Double D, Rennevant rode northward. And because Whitey Hallmark had a rider's frenzied fear of being dragged to death, he walked fast enough to keep a margin of slack in the rope. Walked, and limped, until each staggering step was agony—until the stones he stepped on were like nails driven into his blistered feet.

Twice Hallmark stumbled and fell and scrambled up in panic-prodded haste. It was midafternoon now, with sun glare burning down at full heat, sucking the moisture from Hallmark's sweat-stained shirt. Presently he fell a third time, whereupon Rennevant dismounted.

"Reckon mebbe you know how my hoss felt this morning," he muttered, and turned Hallmark loose.

The Double D foreman had gotten up quickly. But now he sat down. His amber eyes were hot with a futile, festering resentment that was close to turning him berserk. He opened his lips, mumbled, "I'll—

I'll pay—" then clamped them shut again without finishing.

Rennevant grinned. "You'll pay hell," he scoffed and, remembering the handcuffs in his saddle bags, felt tempted to arrest Hallmark there and then. But that would expose him as a badgetoter, and he wasn't ready for that yet.

So he said dryly, "I'll be seeing you again, Whitey. And I'll be teaching you another lesson in manners. You'll be a real educated galoot when I get through with you."

Then Rennevant turned west, circling his back-trail as a precaution against running into the posse. Crossing an open summit, he saw another homestead clearing; another loghouse and corral. A woman in a poke bonnet was spading a garden plot near the house, and a little girl with bright ribbons in her hair was playing with a puppy on the shaded stoop.

Watching that tranquil scene and knowing how hugely range war would change it, Rennevant felt a futile regret. It seemed almost impossible that this country was on the thin edge of bloody conflict—that these hushed hills would soon resound to the crash of guns and the curses of dying men. Yet even at this moment, all the ingredients of hate and greed and violence were in these hills. Five gunhung riders were pushing cattle onto Anvil range; Whitey Hallmark was limping toward the Double D with a bloodlust brew of hate running hot in his veins, and somewhere—perhaps over the next ridge—a three-man posse stalked a rider for murder.

No, there was no peace there. No real peace. Just a temporary hush before the storm; just a little time for playing with puppies on shaded stoops.

Riding on down the slope, Rennevant skirted a meadow where cattle grazed. Instinctively checking their brands, he saw a lot of Double D's, a few Y

Drags, Pot Hooks, and some AE Connected which he guessed was Alex Engle's brand. The Pool cattle were mostly cows and calves; but the Double D's were big steers with vented brands—the unreadable "bug" brands of Old Mexico. Recalling what Anne had told him about the Anvil making a wide wedge between the Homestead Hills and the Border, Rennevant toyed with the suspicion that Diamond Dan Bannerman might want the Anvil for something besides extra grazing ground. If Bannerman was dealing with Mexican cattle thieves, this wedge of range would be a priceless possession for him.

Rennevant was thinking about that when Turk Gallego stepped from behind a windfall with a leveled gun in his hand and said quietly—almost whisperingly, "Don't do anything foolish, friend."

Cursing himself for a careless fool, Rennevant eyed Gallego intently, wondering if Shumway and Haggin were nearby. If they weren't too close, there might be a chance to ride this little man down, for he was less than five feet away.

But even as Rennevant made ready to jab spurs to the roan, Gallego said softly, "Don't do it, friend."

He came all the way out of the windfall, the reins of his bronc looped over his left arm. He eased off to one side, keeping his sharp eyes on Rennevant every instant, not lowering the gun nor relaxing the menace of its aimed muzzle.

There was something strange about his action, and it tugged at the fringes of Rennevant's mind. Gallego could have ambushed him easily, without risk to himself. Right now he could release the gun's hammer and be positive its slug would slam through the Durham sack in Rennevant's shirt pocket. But Turk Gallego was waiting. For what?

Then Turk said something that further puzzled Rennevant. He said, "I don't know what your game is here, friend. But you're living on borrowed time."

Still watching closely, he canted his head as if listening for expected sounds. And in that brief interval a startling thought struck Steve Rennevant— a possible explanation for Gallego's reluctance to end this deal swiftly and brutally, as Red Haggin would have ended it. Or Sheriff Shumway. Pete Modesto had said Gallego was new on Bannerman's payroll. Turk looked tough, and he probably was tough; but he didn't have the vicious look of a cold-blooded killer.

Rennevant relaxed in the saddle. "What," he asked, "does that badge say you're wearing in your pocket?"

Gallego didn't lower the gun. And there was no visible change in the sober mask of his swarthy face when he said, "Border Patrol. What does yours say?"

Rennevant chuckled, knowing now that this little rider had guessed his lawman identity first. "Deputy U. S. Marshal," he drawled, and remembering how strongly Gallego had attracted his attention the night before in the saloon, said amusedly, "You keep strange company, Turk. You do for a fact."

"Got my reasons," Gallego muttered, and lowered the gun. He listened again, then said whisperingly, "Two herds of Sonora steers been smuggled across the line in the last three months. I'm trying to find out when the Double D plans to make another raid into Mexico."

So that was it! This taciturn little lawdog was playing a crafty, waiting game. And a dangerous one. If Bannerman so much as suspected his role, Gallego would die. For that was the penalty a spy always paid, especially a badgetoting spy looking for hangnoose bait. And now, with open range war imminent, Gallego would be a target for Pool guns along with other Double D riders if he continued his masquerade.

"I'm not the only one who's living on borrowed time," Rennevant said. "Hell is going to pop around here soon. The Pool is going on the warpath."

Then he asked, "Want me to tell my friends who you are, so they won't be shooting at you?"

"No," Turk said instantly. "Somebody might talk out of turn. Bannerman is about due to grab another herd of Sonora steers, and I want to get the dead-wood on him his time, come hell or high water. Two of my pardners stopped lead on Bannerman's last raid, and one of them died."

He listened again, then said, "Haggin and Shum-way aren't far off. You'd better make some tracks, friend."

"There's a few things I'm curious about," Renne-vant declared, wanting to know about the ambush deal that had somehow failed to keep Bob Cruzatte from reaching San Sabino.

But Gallego said, "Some other time, friend" and, stepping into saddle, rode up on the slope.

Afterward, as Rennevant crossed a valley with good graze in its bottom, he saw a big bunch of Mexican steers mixed with slab-ribbed Anvil cows and scrawny calves. Keeping tab, he tallied five Double D brands for every Anvil, that ratio diminishing somewhat as he rode farther south. But three to one—even two to one—spelled eventual disaster for Cruzate, who needed every blade of grass to nourish his drought-famished stock. One month of real overcrowding would ravage this range.

No wonder old Jeff had gone loco in San Sabino last night. Without a crew to push Bannerman's cattle back, he had faced sure ruin. And although the Homestead Hills outfits faced the same fate, they had refused to fight. But they were going to fight now, and Rennevant was idly formulating a plan for the coming conflict when he topped a bluff some three miles north of the Anvil.

There he halted, and had his first clear view of Cruzatte's home quarters—seeing a spacious, L-shaped 'dobe house with its gallery facing east. A bunkhouse, several sheds and an array of corrals were separated from the main building by a tri-angular compound. A huge cottonwood obscured one end of the gallery, and twin rows of pepper trees bordered the roadway that skirted a windmill tank on the south side of the house.

It was, Rennevant reflected, a fitting home for a saddle-warped old pioneer. A cow country palace to be proud of; a hard-won heritage to protect against the designs of greedy men. And because he'd been homeless as a stray dog for five rough-and-tumble years, Steve Rennevant felt a sudden sense of lone-liness. That home down there, and the log cabins back in the hills, were symbols of something accomplished—monuments to the men who'd built them. The poorest homesteader had a shack to come back to when the day's riding was done. But what did Steve Rennevant have to show for five years' riding? Just a lot of horse tracks in the dust.

Remembering how Anne had kissed him up there on Sashay Ridge, Rennevant knew abruptly why this urgent sense of lack and loneliness had come at sight of the Anvil. Anne was down there, her presence like a magnet attracting his attention, shaping his thoughts. And it would always be like that. No matter how far a distance lay between them, she would be the one full image of his desire—a constant, unwavering beacon across the long and lonely miles.

For the first time in his life, Steve Rennevant took a look into the future—and grimaced at what he saw. Sooner or later, some noose-dodging thief would beat him to the draw—would pull a sneak shot on him; and even if that didn't happen until he was too old to care, it was a dreary picture. A man could take plenty of pride in the badge he wore, and in reaping retribution for his dead father. But there came a time when pride wasn't enough; when hate and vengeance burned themselves out and only the embers remained. And there came a time when a man wanted a place of his own, with a wife to share it.

Perhaps, he mused, that time had come for him. And there might be another homestead in the hills when his law chore here was finished. A cozy, stout-walled home with curtains at the windows and a blond goddess of a girl to welcome him when the day's riding was done.

At dusk Anne saw Rennevant ride into the yard. She had just taken a pan of biscuits from the oven; she stood at the window for a moment, seeing the ramrod straightness of his tall form in saddle, and feeling a quick surge of relief that he was all right. Then, as the hot pan burned through the towel which protected her hands, she hurriedly deposited the biscuits on the kitchen table.

Her father called a friendly greeting to Rennevant from the gallery, and presently Anne heard the drone of their voices over at the horse corral where Rennevant was unsaddling. Jeff had been somewhat flabbergasted at the news that Mayor Matabelle was going to finance a showdown against the Double D; so surprised and pleased that he'd discarded all his bitter resentment toward the Pool at once. He'd been downright jovial with Jules Larson, and later, when Larson had borrowed a horse and ridden away, her father had called, "We'll show the Double D bunch, Jules—we'll show 'em good and proper!"

Now, Anne guessed, he was telling Rennevant

about the plan he and Larson had discussed: the huge task of hazing Double D stock off Anvil and then cleaning it out of the Homestead Hills. It was almost dark when she went to the door and called, "Come and get it!"

A cool breeze ran down from the Ramparts, and there was a hint of impending storm in the massed clouds above Sashay Ridge. But this lamplit kitchen was a cheerful place, and when Steve Rennevant eased through the door with a grin on his face, it seemed more cheerful here than it had been in months.

He said, "Hello, Anne," and, sniffing the food-scented air, added, "Sure smells good to a hungry man."

"Anne ain't much account in a kitchen," Cruzatte drawled with mock gravity. "But she'll do until I can git a Chinese cook."

Presently, when they were eating, Anne noticed fresh scars on Rennevant's knuckles. Recalling what he'd said about paying Hallmark off with his fists, she nodded at his hands and asked, "Did you meet Whitey?"

"Yeah," Rennevant admitted without enthusiasm.

He seemed reluctant to discuss the details, so Anne didn't press the subject. But he showed no reluctance about eating, nor in his praise when the meal was finished. "Best tasting supper I ever ate, bar none," he declared, almost soberly; and Anne knew he meant it.

"Thank you, sir," she said smilingly, seeing open admiration in his eyes; and something else, something that hadn't shown before—an expression that was close to desire.

Afterwards, while she washed the dishes, Anne listened to Steve and her father discuss ways and means of waging war against the Double D. "First

thing is to git them danged Mex steers off my grass,"
old Jeff announced. "Then we'll chouse 'em out of
the hills."

"You planning to drive them back to Bannerman's
range?" Rennevant inquired, puffing contentedly on
the cigar Jeff had given him.

"Sure—where else would we drive 'em?"

"Well, I've got reason to believe they were smuggled out of Mexico," Rennevant said. "Seems like it
would be easier to drive them south. That way you'd
be doing three jobs at once: you'd be getting shut
of them quicker, Bannerman would be losing them,
and mebbe the rightful owners might get 'em back."

"By grab—I never thought of that!" Cruzatte exclaimed, a quick smile warming his faded eyes.
"Also, there'd be less chance of Double D riders
messin' up our drive."

Rennevant nodded, and presently asked, "How
many men in Bannerman's crew?"

"Eighteen, not counting Fay Shumway. But he's
on the payroll just like the others. In fact, he probably gits higher pay than the rest."

The talk ran on, covering all the angles of armed
conflict; how much ammunition and supplies would
be needed; which men would ride with Rennevant
as roving gun guards while the others worked cattle;
how to meet the showdown fight when it came.

"We'll have twelve men, and mebbe two-three
youngsters who'll do for cow chousin'," Cruzatte
reported. "Seems like we got a real good chance of
winnin'."

"A chance, anyway," Rennevant said. "But licking
the Double D crew may not end the trouble. It's
my hunch you could kill every rider on Bannerman's
payroll and still not win anything more than a short
spell of peace."

Cruzatte didn't agree with that. "Hell's fire," he

exclaimed, "Diamond Dan is just one man. He's only as strong as his crew. Take that away from him and he's finished!"

"Mebbeso," Rennevant said.

But later, when Anne sat with him on the gallery after Jeff had gone to bed, Rennevant voiced his hunch again. "There'll be no real peace in this country until Bannerman leaves it. And I know of only one thing that would make him leave it."

"A bullet?" Anne asked softly.

"Yeah," Rennevant drawled. "A bullet between the eyes."

Then, while a full moon played hide and seek with the high-banked clouds above Sashay Ridge, they talked of other, more pleasant things—and some of it was said without the use of words.

7

AT TEN O'CLOCK that night Sheriff Shumway and Red Haggin rode leg-weary horses into San Sabino and reported to their boss. "Somebody tipped Rennevant off," Shumway declared. "He'd left the livery rig and was on hossback when we went up Sashay Ridge."

"Did you get him?" Bannerman demanded briskly.

The sheriff shook his head, and Haggin said sheepishly, "He hightailed it into the hills."

Bannerman slammed a half-smoked cigar into a cuspidor. "So Rennevant got away again!" he roared. "Three to one, and you let him slide through your goddam fingers!"

"Somebody warned him we was comin'," Shumway alibied.

"What of it?" Bannerman demanded. "You got close enough to see him, didn't you?"

Both men nodded, whereupon Diamond Dan exclaimed, "What the hell you think I'm paying you big wages for—just to fancy-dance through the hills admiring your shadows?"

Then he asked, "Where's Gallego?"

"We split up," Shumway explained, "trying to cut Rennevant's trail. We never did see Turk after that. We even stopped by the ranch, but he didn't show there neither."

Red Haggin said, "Whitey told us Rennevant jumped him from behind, beat hell out of him and took his horse. Whitey's face is a mess, boss. And his feet is blistered all to hell. He can't hardly walk on 'em."

"By God, that's good!" Bannerman shouted. "Half my crew riding the hills, and Rennevant makes monkeys of 'em all!"

Shumway's pride was hurt, and he showed it. But Red Haggin took Bannerman's denunciation with stolid indifference. "Somethin' queer about that Gallego galoot," he said, "Turk had a Winchester in his hands, but he never fired it at Rennevant. He just hit a shuck off through the brush, like mebbe he was tryin' to head Rennevant off. But he didn't do no shootin' at all."

"Say," Shumway exclaimed, "somebody sent word ahead to Rennevant that we was comin' after him—and only us four knew it."

"Yes," Bannerman mused, instantly interested. "Just us four."

He went to the door, opened it and gave the saloon a searching glance. Piano Pete was dealing stud poker to three players—an El Paso whiskey drummer, Fat Foster, the barkeep, and a clerk from the Mercantile. No sign of Gallego.

Bannerman turned to Haggin, and said impatiently, "Go get two fresh horses from the stable. We're riding to the ranch right now."

"How about me?" Shumway asked.

"You stay here, and keep your goddam eyes open," Bannerman snapped. "If Gallego comes in, bring him to the ranch. And if you see Rennevant—shoot him!"

They went out through the saloon to the street then, and the Mercantile clerk said secretively, "Wait until Diamond Dan hears this latest bit of news."

Piano Pete tried to break that talk by raising the pot ten dollars on a jack of hearts. "Come on," he urged, "let's play poker."

But Fat Foster asked, "What news you talking about, Gebbert?"

"Mayor John is backing the Pool with wide open credit," the clerk declared. "Those Hills boys will be well-heeled with bullets from now on."

"You sure about that?" the barkeep demanded.

"Sure I'm sure. I heard Mayor John tell Jules Larson he'd back 'em to the limit—and that this here Rennevant would lead the fight."

Foster pushed back his chair and went out to the stoop at a ponderous, waddling run. But Bannerman was already riding away from the stable with Red Haggin.

Across the street, in the Cattle King Hotel, Doc Dineen came downstairs and found Kate Carmody waiting with an unspoken question in her Irish eyes.

"Anne was right," the medico declared. "Bob won't be crippled, although I can't see how those slugs missed smashing his hip to slivers. He'll be right as rain in no time at all."

Whereupon Kate let out a little squeal of happiness and kissed Doc's pudgy cheek.

Up on Society Hill Mayor Matabelle was playing a final game of dominoes with his wife, and out at

the Double D Turk Gallego gave Whitey Hallmark
a two-word explanation of his late arrival.

"Got lost," the dark-faced little rider said flatly.

During the next forty-eight hours a radical change
took place in the Homestead Hills. Men who had
advertised their peaceful intention by riding unarmed for months suddenly sprouted Colt-filled
holsters. They rode with a new look in their eyes.
Even their talk was different, taking on the aggres-
sive tone of fighting men. And although their women-
folk watched this change with dread and foreboding,
more than one wife looked upon her husband with
new respect.

In less than two day's time the Pool-Anvil combination was completely organized and men were riding toward the appointed meeting place with extra
horses for the grueling job ahead. From West Creek
and Blackjack Canyon they came; from Burnt
Meadow and Sombrero Butte and the Pot Holes—
all heading for Jules Larson's J Bar L. Here, at the
northern fringe of the Homestead Hills, the drive
would start; and here Steve Rennevant's roving patrol against Double D raiders would make its head-
quarters.

Soon after sun-up of the second day, Rennevant
hazed ten broncs northward from Anvil. Behind
him, in the ranch yard, Anne Cruzatte helped her
father hook a four-horse hitch to the chuckwagon.
Jeff was going to San Sabino for provisions and
would reach the J Bar L some time before dark.
Anne, despite her urgent desire to "make a hand at
the round-up," was going to remain in town with
her brother Bob.

When Rennevant rimmed the mesa north of Anvil
he glanced back and saw Anne wave to him. He
couldn't distinguish her features from that distance,

but he knew she'd be smiling and he knew exactly how the smile would curve her lips and fashion twin dimples in her cheeks. And so he grinned, and rode on across the mesa like a man with pictures in his mind, and five hours later choused the broncs into Larson's corral.

Alex Engle and his wife had already arrived. When the young husband tried to thank Rennevant for "stompin' that low-livered snake Hallmark," Rennevant said, "Can't use any thanks, Alex—but I could use a guide for a looksee at the range north of here."

"Sure," Engle said eagerly. "I'll be proud to show you. And I know a perfect lookout spot, for keeping tabs on the Double D."

Whereupon he proved it by taking Rennevant up the brush-tangled summit above Pyramid Pass—northern gateway to the hills.

Soon after they'd ridden off, Ed Wales arrived. Then Ollie Shannon rode in with his two teenage sons, and an hour later Jim Highbaugh, Luke Yancey and Sam Stoval came, driving eight loose broncs ahead of them. Late in the afternoon Jeff Cruzatte wheeled into the yard with the Anvil chuckwagon piled high with provisions, extra Winchesters and ammunition.

"Makes a man feel young again," he declared grinningly, and shook hands with men he hadn't spoken to for months.

Soon after that Gabe Lee, oldest settler in the hills, rode in with his son-in-law, broad-chested Pete Meadows, and they were soon followed by the two Logan brothers, who completed the Pool membership.

At dusk, when Rennevant returned with Engle, he glanced reflectively at the campfire where Mrs. Larson and her daughter were helping old Gabe Lee prepare a chuckwagon supper. The smell of Dutch-oven cooking made him remember the last round-up he'd ridden with his father, back in Texas seven years before. There'd been no hate in him then, nor any notches on his gun; nor any sense of loneliness.

Rennevant was thinking about that when Jeff Cruzatte called, "Come on over here where the boys can git a look at you, Steve," and ushered Rennevant into the circle of firelight. "Here's our gun boss—the gent who made Bannerman's slug slammers shiver in their boots!"

Rennevant's face turned ruddy. An old resentment stirred in him, and for a long moment he stood moodily silent. Every man in the group seemed to be looking at him as if he were some sort of a gunslick freak.

"Tell us how you want the work done," Jules Larson invited.

Rennevant shook his head. "The brush popping is up to you and Jeff," he said bluntly. "Give me four men, and I'll try to keep Bannerman's bunch from interfering with your work."

"Who you want to ride with you?" Alex Engle asked, eagerness brightening his eyes.

"You, for one," Rennevant said. Then he chose lean, lantern-jawed Jim Highbaugh; Luke Yancey, who was also on the lean, long-geared side; and big Pete Meadows.

"It's going to be rough," Rennevant warned them. "I'd like that understood right now."

Ollie Shannon asked, "You reckon we're goin' to cut the mustard?"

Rennevant shrugged. "Mebbe yes—mebbe no," he muttered and, realizing that some of the men probably wouldn't live to see the round-up completed, added soberly, "It'll take some doing."

"A tol'able lot of doin'," Gabe Lee called from across the campfire.

"And a lot of dying," Mrs. Larson prophesied.

For a long moment then, as her words cast their spell on the group, there was a thoughtful silence. It occurred to Rennevant that most of these men had never drawn a gun against another man. No wonder they'd been afraid to buck Bannerman's gunslick riders; no wonder they'd waited until there seemed no other way of survival. And now that they'd decided to fight, what chance would they have?

As if in answer to that question, there was a rushing thud of hard-run horses at the edge of the clearing and a man's high-pitched yell: "Here comes company!"

"Get away from the fire," Rennevant warned at once, and heard a horse slide in a swerving turn.

Then, as another horse drifted into the yard, the first one went charging back into the woods, its hoof pound rapidly diminishing.

Rennevant peered at the oncoming bronc. The animal stopped ten yards away, breathing hard and letting out a nervous snort as Rennevant moved toward it.

"Easy, boy," Rennevant soothed it, and wondered why this riderless animal had been deliberately hazed into the yard. Then, as his eyes focused to the darkness, he saw the vague shape of something slung across the saddle—and guessed what it was!

Jules Larson said worriedly, "One of them rode back into the woods."

And Jeff Cruzatte asked, "Who is it, Steve?"

"Turk Gallego," Rennevant muttered and, leading the bronc into the firelight, saw that his guess had been correct.

Gallego's hands and feet were tied to opposite stirrups, his head dangling grotesquely. The back of his shirt was stained a reddish brown between the shoulders and there was a Border Patrol badge pinned there. Blood ran down his neck, making gruesome patterns on his loose-jawed face.

Shock ran its quick course through these men; it held them in stiff astonishment. From the yonder gloom came a taunting, long-drawn laugh that ended with an obscene chuckle and another rush of fading hoof beats.

"Shot in the back!" Jules Larson exclaimed.

"Who's shot in the back?" Mrs. Larson demanded excitedly.

She elbowed her way through the ring of silent men, took one brief look and turned hastily back to the Dutch ovens.

"Don't look, Ruth," she warned. "It's—it's awful!"

Afterward, when Turk's body had been buried and Steve Rennevant was fashioning a wooden cross to mark the grave, old Gabe Lee called, "Come and git it, you rannies. No use to let a buryin' spoil your appetite for vittles."

Whereat one of the Logan brothers picked up his tin plate and drawled, "It ain't like Gallego was a friend of our'n. Let's eat hearty ag'in' the hard work tomorrow."

Which was, Rennevant knew, an entirely practical suggestion. But although he ate with the others and joined in their discussion of the task ahead, he couldn't shake off the morbid memory of that law badge pinned to the back of Turk's bloody shirt. Any one of the Double D crew might have murdered Gallego, but only Diamond Dan Bannerman would have contrived that final gesture of derision for an honest lawman.

Rennevant was still thinking about that when he crawled into his blankets over by the horse corral. There seemed to be a remote warning in the fact that Bannerman had pinned a badge to Turk's shirt.

But Rennevant couldn't figure out what the warning might be.

For a time then, his thoughts turned to Anne—how she'd sat beside him on the gallery the night before, the scent of her hair making an intimate perfume that blended with the moonlight. She'd seemed surprised when he'd told her about his dream of having a home. She'd smiled and said, "I didn't think that drifters dreamed of anything so substantial as a home."

He had been on the point of telling her about his badge; about wanting to corral the Hallmark gang and quit the law game for keeps. But instead he'd kissed her—last night, at just about this time.

Rennevant grinned, remembering. But presently he got to thinking about Gallego again, wondering if Turk had also dreamed of having a home. Little Turk, who'd looked tough as Texas whang.

Abruptly then, Rennevant understood what the warning was that had evaded him. That badge pinned to Turk's shirt meant that Dan Bannerman was at the Double D. The rider who'd hazed the corpse-laden bronc into the yard must have seen the group at the campfire; he'd tell his boss, and that might mean a raid—*tonight!*

Even as these successive links of evidence formed into a hunch. Rennevant got to his feet. And because hunches had always been his bugle call to action, he went to the corral and roped a horse.

"Where you goin'?" Jim Highbaugh called from his blankets.

"Pyramid Pass," Rennevant said.

Highbaugh got out of his blankets. "Mind if I go along?"

And young Alex Engle, sitting with his wife on the front stoop, asked quickly, "Me too?"

Rennevant said, "Sure," and when Pete Meadows

and Luke Yancey also came to the corral, he added grinningly, "Sure don't take much to organize a moonlight ride in this outfit."

Other men were stirring in their blankets now. Jeff Cruzatte declared sleepily, "Double D won't bother us tonight, Steve. They don't even know what we're up to yet."

"Bannerman might make a good guess," Rennevant drawled and, riding across the yard with his four companions, said, "You'd best get your sleep and let us do the nighthawking."

Ruth Engle ran out to her husband and kissed him good-bye and said nervously, "Be careful, Alex."

"Sure—sure," the young rider agreed, plainly embarrassed by this show of emotion. When he caught up with Rennevant at the edge of the yard he said scoffingly, "Women-folks always worrying."

"Mebbe they've got reason to worry," Rennevant suggested.

But later, when they'd scouted Pyramid Pass and Rennevant rode alone to the crest of its high western wall, he was beginning to think Cruzatte's opinion was correct. A full moon flooded the northern desert with blue-white light and only the shadow of greasewood and an occasional suguaro cactus showed against the moon-silvered dust.

Rennevant picked out the far-off twinkle of the Double D's lighted windows and was on the verge of riding back down to the pass when that faint illumination disappeared. At first he thought the lamp over there had been blown out, but a moment later the light appeared again—and again went out.

Whereupon Rennevant dismounted and, hunkering on his heels, began a patient probing of the moonlit flats. Somebody was moving in front of that distant lamp. It might be a man walking in the ranch yard, passing back and forth in front of the window. Or it might be a group of riders coming that way.

"See anything?" Pete Meadows called up from the pass.

Rennevant didn't answer at once. He kept scanning the desert's floor; kept trying to discover some sign of movement between the scattered shadows of greasewood and saluting suguaros. That distant pinpoint of window light showed without interruption now. The Double D, he reflected, kept late hours for a cow outfit.

Then abruptly he saw something move out there on the desert—something that looked like the strungout shadow of a tall cactus. He stepped over to the rim of the pass and said quietly, "They're coming. Too far away to tell how many, but looks like five, six riders. Mebbe more."

"You sure they're coming this way?" Alex Engle asked excitedly.

Rennevant nodded and, deciding at once how this game should be played, gave his four-man crew instructions for their first fight. "Alex, you take the horses back to the south end of the pass and tie them so they won't break away when the shooting starts. Then come up here with me. The rest of you spread out along the east wall, and keep out of sight. When the Double D gets close enough I'll tell them they can't go through here."

"You reckon they'll take your word for it?" Luke Yancey inquired.

"No," Rennevant said and, leading his bronc into the brush, tied it securely to a scrub oak.

Presently, when the three men on the east wall had forted themselves up behind boulders and Alex Engle had joined him on the crest, Rennevant took a more accurate tally of the oncoming riders. They were still too far away to show individually, but they were riding strung out and he judged their number to be upwards of a dozen men. It occurred to him now that Bannerman wouldn't send so large a force just to scout out the reason for the gathering at the J Bar L. A couple of riders would have done for that kind of detail. The size of this group meant just one thing—the planned, cold-blooded massacre of sleeping men at the J Bar L!

The Double D bunch were getting closer now. Close enough to count. "Fourteen men!" Alex Engle exclaimed whisperingly.

"Yeah," Rennevant muttered, taking stock of his position as a gambler might judge cards in a game of stud. The odds here were problematical, depending less on numbers than on the qualities involved. Five seasoned fighting men should easily hold this pass against fourteen raiders. But he didn't have seasoned fighters. All he had was four homesteaders clutching Winchesters in sweaty hands. If they spooked in the pinch, or if excited shaking spoiled too many of their shots, the Double D would charge through the pass. And even though Bannerman's grisly plan of massacre would be thwarted by the far-reaching echo of blasting guns, the raiders could turn the J Bar L into a bloody place of death and destruction.

Rennevant was thinking about that when he saw the Double D crew pull to a stop. Even as he watched this obvious consultation, Rennevant guessed what the next move would be, and had his strong hunch that Diamond Dan was out there in that compact group of riders.

"What'd they stop for?" Engle asked.

"Because they're wondering if we had sense enough to guard this pass tonight," Rennevant muttered. "In a minute now you'll see a couple of riders come on ahead."

And so they did.

Rennevant smiled. He felt certain now that Dan Bannerman was running this deal. It would be like the big schemer to play it safe, even with thirteen hired gunhawks riding with him. Diamond Dan had a cautious man's habit of looking around all the corners, and this trait might give the Pool men the one thing they needed most right now—a chance to get some gun-savvy before a showdown battle materialized. They needed a little time to tromp down their nervousness; to get the feel of shooting, and of being shot at.

Rennevant hunkered in the shadow of a huge boulder near the rim of the pass. He watched the two riders come warily up the steep rise to the entrance, and felt his pulse pound faster and harder, the way it always did just before a fight. Sweat trickled from his arm pits, feeling cold against his flesh, and there was a familiar tightness in his chest. All this was the usual and inevitable tension of waiting—of knowing that each move from now on had to be made in its proper order.

The riders came steadily forward, and when they were so close that he had to stand up to see them over the rim, Rennevant fired a single shot, that bullet stirring a tendril of moonlit dust directly ahead of their horses.

Both riders stopped, and Rennevant called, "Turn around, boys. This trail is closed."

"Who says so?" one of them demanded.

Rennevant moved out of the shadow, making himself a plain target. "I say so," he declared.

A man back in the main group exclaimed, "That's Rennevant!"

And someone punctuated that exclamation with a rifle blast.

This hastily fired shot missed Rennevant by a wide

margin. He dodged behind the boulder, and at that moment all those yonderly guns opened up at once, their concentrated fire lacing the crest with a vibrating whang and whine of searching slugs.

Keeping low, Rennevant eased over to the rim in time to see the two riders start into the pass. He fired, and missed. Or so he thought. But before he could send a second shot into the pass he saw one rider jump from a wild-pitching mount and knew his first slug had hit the horse. The dismounted rider jumped up behind his companion; they turned back, saw the Double D bunch charging forward, and turned again, both firing up at Rennevant.

All this in the space of a few fleeting seconds—in the time it took those three Pool men on the east wall to get their Winchesters into action. Then, as Bannerman's bunch galloped forward, believing the pass was guarded by one lone sentinel, the guns of Highbaugh, Yancey and Meadows began blasting. And though this outburst of shooting was far from accurate, it disrupted the Double D charge at once. Surprised raiders broke ino a dust-hazed tangle of cursing men and whirling horses. They fanned out in wild confusion, firing random shots at the muzzle flare above them, until Dan Bannerman bellowed, "Back! Ride back!"

Hearing that bull-toned voice, Rennevant tried to identify Bannerman. If Diamond Dan could be chopped down now, the whole picture would change. If the greedy rangehog who'd planned a ruthless slaughter of sleeping men could be killed here tonight, there'd be peace in the Homestead Hills!

Eagerly, with his Winchester cocked and ready for instant aiming, Rennevant peered at the shifting shapes below him. But the dust was too thick to allow more than a hazy impression as the riders galloped away from the pass.

Big Pete Meadows yelled, "Dab it on 'em, Pool!"

And presently, when Bannerman's bunch was out of range, Luke Yancey bragged, "We got two of the dirty sons, anyway!"

Rennevant grinned. These men had been rank amateurs at the gun game an hour ago. Now they'd had the stink of powdersmoke in their nostrils and the whine of bullets in their ears. Their baptism of fire was over.

It occurred to him then that Alex Engle's gun had gone strangely quiet. And remembering how the Double D had raked this summit with that first volley, he felt a sudden stab of apprehension. If young Alex had been killed—

Turning quickly, Rennevant scanned the summit, and saw no sign of Engle. "Alex," he called, genuinely alarmed. "Alex!"

For a moment there was no answer, and in that interval Rennevant flinched at the thought of facing Ruth Engle, of having to tell her that Alex was dead —that her husband's death was the price paid for tonight's victory.

Then Engle said, "Over here," and Rennevant saw him sitting behind a boulder—staring at his blood-stained right arm.

Rennevant ran over to him hastily examined the wound which was just above the elbow, and used his neckerchief to fashion a tourniquet. "Why didn't you tell me you'd stopped a slug?" he asked.

Engle stood up, white-faced and shaky. "I got sick," he admitted, and went into a spasm of retching.

8

FOR FIVE CONSECUTIVE days, while Rennevant's riders kept constant vigil, the round-up crew worked from dawn until dark, unmolested. In high spirits over the Pyramid Pass fight and the good progress they were making, Cruzatte's brush-popping brigade rode like men racing against time; like men making a vital crusade. And so they were.

Three times during this period Double D riders had been seen in the hills, and quickly chased out. But aside from these one-man scouting forays, there'd been no action, and that fact puzzled Steve Rennevant.

That defeat would be a bitter pill for so proud a tyrant to swallow, Rennevant guessed. But being a surething schemer, Diamond Dan was swallowing it instead of chancing another ambush. The thought occurred to Rennevant that Bannerman probably didn't know about the round-up, and so believed the full strength of the Pool was guarding the hills against invasion. But even so, it seemed uncommon strange that a big gunhawk outfit like the Double D should wait so long before striking again.

Five days of waiting, and watching, and long riding. Five nights while the fat full moon shrank slowly, its light fading a little more each night. Then, just after dawn of the sixth day, rain began to fall. Not hard, in the way of summer rains that slash down just long enough to start flash floods. But a slow drizzle that dripped steadily from low-hanging clouds. A typical rain, two months ahead of schedule.

Rennevant was relieving sleepy-eyed Alex Engle on the lookout perch atop Pyramid Pass when the first drops began to fall. He glanced out across the gloom-shrouded desert and said thoughtfully, "This might be what Bannerman has been waiting for."

"Why?" Engle asked, absently rubbing his bandaged arm, which was healed enough to itch. "What difference does a little rain make?"

Rennevant pointed to a mist-filled arroyo north of the pass. "That's the way these hills will be in another hour. We won't be able to see half a mile away, even from here. And there'll be no dust to tell us when riders cross the desert."

"Gosh!" Engle exclaimed, then asked, "Want me to stay with you, Steve—in case they make a try?"

Rennevant shook his head. "One man is all we can spare here," he said, peering toward the Double D, which was entirely hidden by drizzling rain and fog. "There's other places they can sneak through without being seen today, and I've got a hunch that's the way Bannerman will do it—send riders through three or four different places at the same time."

"How we goin' to stop 'em?" Engle asked, apprehension replacing his sleepiness.

Rennevant shaped up a smoke. He peered out at the desert again, his hunch of impeding calamity growing stronger and stronger. This was the day, all right. The day Bannerman had been waiting for. Diamond Dan wouldn't pass up a chance like this, with everything in his favor.

"Go tell Luke Yancey to hightail it over to Blackjack Canyon and fort up for a fight," he said finally. "Tell Meadows to do the same at West Creek, and send Highbaugh to Pot Hole Gap."

"How about me?" Engle asked. "I'm wide awake now, Steve. I don't need no sleep."

Rennevant grinned. "You won't get any," he said.

Grab yourself a cup of coffee at Larson's, then ride to the round-up camp. They should be close to Spanish Flats by now, and easy to locate. Tell the crew I figger the hills will be full of Double D riders by noon, and they'd best guard their homes."

"Gosh—you think it's going to be that bad?" Engle asked, climbing into saddle.

Rennevant nodded and, watching this young rider go hastily down the slope, wondered if the orders he'd just given would be delivered in time. There wasn't any way to keep the Double D out of these fog-bound hills. But if Bannerman's bunch could be delayed—if Yancey, Meadows and Highbaugh could hold them long enough—the round-up crew might save their homes. For that, he was sure, was what this fight would become today: a desperate attempt to ward off kill-crazy hellions bent on destroying every home in the hills.

It was a dismal thought. It kept pressing down on him like the heavy clouds that sagged lower and lower, until their gray wetness enveloped the summit completely. Whereupon Rennevant had another hunch—and climbed quickly into the saddle.

Two hours later, at Blackjack Canyon.

Luke Yancey hunkered on his heels behind a rock outcrop, trying to roll a cigarette and cursing softly when rain dripped from the turned-down brim of his battered hat, spoiling the cigarette. He took out a fresh paper, and was fashioning another smoke when he glanced along the mist-blurred canyon and saw five riders loom darkly against the gray drizzle.

Pure panic gripped Luke Yancey. The tobacco sack slid from his fingers and the thought flashed through his mind that there wasn't a chance to stop all those oncoming riders. Not five of them. Five gunslick fighters. They were too close. They'd cut him down before he fired his second shot. No, there wasn't a chance—not a goddam ghost of a chance!

But Luke Yancey grabbed up his rifle in shaking, sweat-wet hands. He fired, and missed, and fired again, before the first of those yonderly guns began blasting back at him—before a cursing rider howled, "Git that bastard! Git him quick!"

Abruptly then the panic left Luke Yancey. He scarcely flinched when a slug *whanged* so close that it vibrated in his ears. Levering out spent shells, he took time to aim, and heard his own hysterical laughter when one of those riders fell backwards from the saddle. He fired again and saw a horse go down. But the man wasn't hurt; he landed on his feet, gun in hand, and Yancey recognized him by his big buck teeth. Red Haggin.

The blocky redhead was down on one knee, aiming deliberately. His slug came close—closer than any of the others had come. Yancey tried to target him. But the hammer clicked on an empty. He reached inside his slicker for his holster gun, and felt a queer, thudding blow high in his chest; an impact so tremendous that it knocked him off his feet. He felt himself falling. And then he didn't feel anything at all.

West Creek, at almost the same moment.

Big Pete Meadows tied his sweat-lathered bronc to a tree just south of the ford. He was pulling his Winchester from its scabbard when he heard horses splash through the creek ten yards away. Yanking the gun free, he whirled and saw misty shapes come charging down on him.

Muzzle flame made orange flares against the gloom as slugs shrieked past him. He fired point-blank and saw a horse keel completely over, crushing its rider. He tried to dodge behind a windfall; but a

bullet knocked his right leg from under him and he
fell flat. He heard Whitey Hallmark snarl, "Shoot him
again for luck," and his back muscles quivered until
the shot came. Then a gusty sigh slid from his lips.

Pete Meadows lay dead in the mud.

Two miles south of Pot Hole Gap, before noon.

Jim Highbaugh rode a plodding bronc through
hock-high gumbo. This, he reflected, was a hell of a
place to be riding today. Mud holes deep enough to
drown in, and fog so thick you could use it for a pil-
low. Adjusting his slicker against the constant drizzle, he thought about his wife and three kids
—wondered if their roof was leaking. And wished
he'd taken time to fix it before he left home.

Which was when he glimpsed movement in the
murk ahead. A rider momentarily outlined against
a chalky shaft of rock. Then another—and another,
sliding into successive mud holes and bobbing up
again. Five or six riders at least!

Highbaugh whirled his horse off the trail. They
hadn't seen him yet. They weren't expecting Pool
riders this far west. If he eased off into the brush
now they'd never see him. He thought about his wife
and kids again—the roof that needed fixing. Hell, he
wouldn't stand a chance here. If he had reached the
Gap in time to fort up, there would have been a fighting chance at least. But not now.

Whereupon he cursed, and cocked his gun. Those
oncoming raiders would ride him down, he guessed;
but there'd be some empty saddles before they did it.

Gambling on his hunch that Bannerman would
ignore Pyramid Pass and use one or more of the
remote portals, Steve Rennevant headed for Pot Hole
Gap. He was, he judged, less than a mile behind Jim
Highbaugh, who'd left a plain trail all the way from
the J Bar L. Remembering how downright spooky

Highbaugh had been on night patrols, Rennevant kept a sharp lookout ahead. It wouldn't do to over- take Jim too abruptly.

Once he thought he glimpsed a rider going around a brush-fringed turn ahead of him. He called, "Jim," and halted. But there was no answer. He went on, rounding the bend and seeing no sign of movement in the short lane of visibility ahead.

Then, with no warning at all, a rifle's sharp re- port ripped through the fog—close enough to startle Rennevant's bronc. Rennevant drew his gun; he was trying to tally the exact location of that single shot when three more explosions came in quick succes- sion. He caught a glimpse of phantom shapes sliding through the fog-draped brush over to the left—and distinctly heard a man yell, "Swing around him! Circle him!"

Rennevant fired at that voice. He jumped his horse ahead, wanting to break up that forming cir- cle. But the bronc slipped in the mud and went to its knees, and in that same instant a slug smashed Rennevant's right thigh with a force that knocked him half out of saddle.

Shock spiraled through him in one painless, numb- ing wave. It struck his stomach with a momentary sickness that made him gag, and for a queerly sus- pended interval he was unaware of sound or move- ment. Then he felt the horse struggle to its feet and was remotely surprised to find himself still mounted; glad to feel the familiar weight of a gun in his hand.

All the roundabout guns were blasting now. They were making orange slobbers against the gloom. Ren- nevant fired at those brief beacons; he rode around a deep pot hole and fired, and moved again, trying to calculate Highbaugh's position by the rapid shift of firing. He crossed a bank-full creek and saw three riderless horses quartering toward the trail. Jim, he guessed, was still alive—still taking his toll. But Jim was being flanked by that forming circle. If only there was some way to join him—

Abruptly then Rennevant whirled his horse. He headed the three broncs and turned them and yelled, "Come on, Pool!"

Then, with hoof-tossed mud splashing against his face and half blinding him, Rennevant chased the broncs headlong through the brush—whooping and firing—making enough noise for a dozen hell-for-leather riders.

Jim Highbaugh heard that yell, and heard the oncoming commotion. But it didn't make sense to him. The round-up crew couldn't possibly have got up there so soon, and neither could Rennevant. Yet that was Rennevant's voice; it came again and again, in a high rebel yell!

Thoroughly mystified, Highbaugh fired his last remaining shot at two riders whirling their horses in sudden retreat. He plucked fresh shells from his belt with trembling fingers and, knowing how close the margin had been between living and dying, laughed hysterically as three riderless broncs splashed past with Rennevant at their heels.

"Steve!" he called and, watching Rennevant pull up, exclaimed dazedly, "I'll be teetotally damnded!"

"Had a hunch those dudes would spook," Rennevant drawled.

He wiped mud from his eyes, then gave his blood-soaked leg a thoughtful inspection. The bullet was still in there; it made a core of throbbing pain each time he moved the leg.

Highbaugh rode up beside him, glanced at the blood, and blurted, "Hell, you're shot! You're bleeding like a stuck hog!"

"Yeah," Rennevant agreed. "Damn if I ain't."

Afterward, when Highbaugh had used his neckerchief to tie a tourniquet above the wound, Rennevant climbed clumsily into saddle. "Don't reckon it'll stay put long," he muttered. "But it'll save me some blood while it lasts."

They rode back up the trail, stopping at intervals to listen, and hearing nothing behind them. But later, when they reached the West Creek fork, they saw where several horses had churned the muddy trail ahead.

"Bunch got by Pete Meadows," Rennevant muttered and, spurring his jaded bronc into a run, added instinctively, "Poor Pete."

Then, as they neared Sam Stoval's place, the pungent odor of burning tarpaper came to them. Smoke lay thick across the clearing; it billowed sluggishly from the smouldering walls of a flame-gutted cabin, and hovered above a wagon shed where Mrs. Stoval stood with her four-year-old daughter.

"They used our own coal oil to make the house burn," the woman said dejectedly. "They smashed all the spokes out of our wagon and shot the team. Whitey Hallmark knocked me down when I tried to save our blankets."

The little girl wore a wilted red ribbon in her hair. Her chubby face was streaked with tears. "They shooted my puppy," she wailed. "They shooted him dead."

Remembering how he'd seen the little girl playing with her puppy a week before, Rennevant cursed whisperingly. Then he asked, "Which way did they go, ma'am?"

"South," she said, glancing at Jim Highbaugh. "Towards your place, Jim."

Those words struck Highbaugh like a physical blow. They put a wild, frightened look in his eyes, and he blurted, "I'm leavin', Steve—I'm leavin' right now!"

Rennevant nodded and, riding with him, said, "Mebbe we'll get there in time, Jim."

But presently, as they galloped through the darkening woods, they heard shooting ahead—a concentrated burst, then scattering shots that soon ceased entirely.

"Your wife have a gun?" Rennevant asked, punishing his mount to keep up with Highbaugh.

Highbaugh nodded. He cursed through clenched teeth, and said, "She'd make a stand, Mary would. She'd try to save our home."

Then, just before they reached the clearing, Jeff Cruzatte came loping down the road with Gabe Lee and Ed Wales. "We jumped a bunch at your place," Jeff told Highbaugh. "We killed two and drove the others off."

"Thank God!" Highbaugh exclaimed, riding on.

"Where now?" Ed Wales asked wearily.

As if in answer, there was a remote rattle of gunfire off to the east.

"That'll be Ollie Shannon's place," Cruzatte declared, spurring his bronc into a run.

Pitched battles at Shannon's ranch and at the J Bar L. Running fights on timbered ridges and across grassy meadows. Until the last Double D raider had finally slunk out of the hills, and Jeff Cruzatte shouted, "We've licked 'em—by grab! We've busted Bannerman's crew to smithereens!"

And so they had. The bodies of eight Double D riders were already tallied when Steve Rennevant started for town an hour after daylight. But because Bannerman wasn't included in that grisly harvest, there was little satisfaction in the victory for Rennevant. Riding to summon Doc Dineen, he kept hearing the pain-prodded groans of Ollie Shannon, who'd been shot in the side—the monotonous cursing of Gabe Lee, who had a slug-shattered hip.

And presently, when weakness from loss of blood made him grip the saddle for support, Rennevant recalled how big Pete Meadows had looked in the soggy dawn, and Luke Yancey lying dead with little pools of rain water in his sightless eyes.

A dismal victory . . .

9

STEVE RENNEVANT didn't remember much of that ride to San Sabino. The sun broke through the clouds, warming his cold body, drying his mud-spattered clothing. But the sunlight hurt his eyes, so that he could scarcely keep them open. He was tired; more tired than he'd ever been.

Once he noticed that the tourniquet had slipped and that his wound was bleeding again. He thought about stopping to fix it. But there wasn't time. He had to tell Doc Dineen about Ollie Shannon and old Gabe Lee.

Rennevant spurred the lagging bronc, and winced at the splinter of pain that stabbed his leg. He thought about Rowdy then, wondering if the sorrel was still lame. They'd make a good pair now—lame horse and lame rider. It occurred to him that Whitey Hallmark hadn't been tallied with the dead this morning, and that gave him a peculiar sense of satisfaction. For Whitey was his personal target; Whitey, who maimed honest horses and slapped decent women around.

Then he got to thinking about Anne; how soft and sweet her lips were when she smiled—how her voice and her eyes and the feminine fragrance of her hair made magic in the moonlight. He was still thinking of Anne when Hook Hooligan's startled voice demanded, "What the hell happened to ye, lad?"

Rennevant opened his eyes. He had a blurred, queerly distorted vision of Hook, standing in the livery doorway. He tried to rub the red haze out of his eyes—to focus them against the sun's blinding glare. But they wouldn't focus properly.

He said, "Tell Doc Dineen he's needed at Larson's place *muy pronto*," and got stiffly down from the saddle.

Anne Cruzatte was crossing the Cattle King lobby on her way back to the kitchen with Bob's breakfast tray when Hook Hooligan came rushing across the porch and demanded, "Is Doc upstairs?"

Anne nodded, and said, "He's going to unstrap Bob's ribs."

Then, as Hook ran to the stairway, she saw the bloodstains on his shirt sleeve. "What's happened?" she demanded.

"Rennevant's shot," he blurted, rushing up the stairs. "I toted him into my tackroom."

For a single instant, while the significance of those words slugged through her, Anne stood rigidly still. Steve shot? But she'd heard no shooting.

Then she put the tray on a chair. She ran out to the porch and down the street. It didn't occur to her that she was wearing her bedroom slippers—until she lost one. She didn't stop to retrieve it; she didn't notice the astonished expression on Banker Kiley's face, nor hear him exclaim, "What's the rush, Anne?"

All she heard was Hooligan's excited voice saying: "*Rennevant's shot . . . Rennevant's shot!*" Over and over, like a jabbering chant. Until finally she was kneeling over the cot in Hook's tackroom—seeing Steve's beard-bristled face; seeing how gaunt and tired he looked with his eyes closed. And how strangely pale he was. Steve, who'd always been so darkly tanned.

Then she saw his blood-soaked leg and the loose tourniquet. Hastily pulling the soggy neckerchief above the wound, she twisted it tight, using all her strength, and feeling blood's wetness against her fingers. Steve's blood . . .

She was still holding tight to the tourniquet when Doc Dineen came puffing into the tackroom. "You've got to save him," she declared. "Don't let him die, Doc. Please!"

The old medico peered at Rennevant and asked, "Is that the only place he got it—in the leg?"

Anne nodded, whereat Dineen scoffed, "Leg wounds don't kill drifters. Just slows 'em down, is all."

"But he's so pale, Doc—and he's unconscious," Anne insisted.

Dineen opened his medical kit, and said reassuringly, "He's lost a little blood and a lot of sleep. Now if you'll fetch me some hot water from Estevan's Cafe, I'll promise to have this jigger walking within a week."

And five days later, when the old medico lifted the bandage from Rennevant's leg, he said with professional pride, "Looks fine, son. Real fine."

"Yeah," Rennevant muttered. "Pretty as a picture."

Then he asked, "How's Ollie Shannon making it, Doc?"

"Good," Dineen said, "and so's old Gabe. But I lost another patient at the Double D. Buckshot Smith died last night. They say he killed half a dozen men while he was tending bar in Tombstone, but he sure hated to die himself. He cried like a baby."

"So," Rennevant mused, and, watching Doc rebandage his wound, asked, "When do I start walking?"

Dineen eyed him narrowly. "Well, if you'd use a crutch you could start today. But a right-hand crutch might be a trifle awkward in a gun fight."

"Yeah," Rennevant agreed. "It sure would."

"Better stay off your feet another couple days, just to make sure. No use busting that hole open, just because you're tired of Hook's tackroom."

Rennevant grinned, "Not a bad place, at that. Only one door to watch."

The old medico went out then, and Rennevant watched his shadow slide across the barn doorway. He had watched plenty of shadows these past few days, and kept his gun handy all the time. Especially when old Hook was over at the cafe, or back in the barn attending to horses. Bannerman's bunch had shrunk considerably; only four able-bodied riders left, according to Doc Dineen. But Diamond Dan was back in town; so were Whitey Hallmark and Red Haggin.

For a time, while he listened to foot steps on the board sidewalk and kept a strict watch on the door, Rennevant allowed his mind to take another looksee into the future. His part of the Pool fight was over. He'd made a reckless bargain and, in keeping it, had luckily survived. Up to now, at least. And although he knew the next shadow in the doorway might be that of Sheriff Shumway, or Red Haggin, come to take vengeance on a bedfast cripple, he felt no apprehension on that score. Come one, come all, he'd be ready. For there was nothing wrong with his right arm.

But beyond that, he wasn't so sure. He had come to this country to arrest a thief and, failing that, had made a definite deal to round up the Whitey Hallmark gang. That job had to be finished before he could turn in his badge; before he could ask Anne to marry him. And the job might take a lot of doing.

He wondered if there was a letter for him at the post office. And hearing Anne's familiar footsteps on the sidewalk, he felt a quick surge of anticipation —which wasn't entirely for the dinner tray she was bringing to him. She'd spent a lot of time with him lately. But not enough. Twenty-four hours would scarcely be enough, the way he felt about her.

"Hello, patient," she greeted him cheerfully.

Her face was slightly flushed from her walk through the noonday's heat. She smiled and placed the tray expertly on his blanketed knees and let him have a kiss before she straightened up. Then she eyed him critically and said, "You aren't fattening up a bit, Steve. You still look slatty as a starving steer."

"Couldn't you make it a starving horse?" Rennevant teased.

Afterward, when she picked up the tray, he said, "One more noon trip; then you lose your job. I'll be eating my supper at the cafe tomorrow night."

"Did Doc agree to that?" she demanded.

Rennevant nodded, whereupon Anne said, "You men are all alike. Bob is threatening to get out of bed. He can't wait to get down into the street—and get himself shot again."

"Don't blame him much. A man gets jittery, Anne —bunked down all the time."

"But it's not just jitters with Bob," she explained. "He wants to get back the money he lost the day he was ambushed. The two thousand dollars he was bringing home."

"That's a lot of money," Rennevant reflected.

"But not enough to die for," Anne declared and, turning to the doorway, said, "See you at supper time, Steve."

Two thousand dollars.

Two thousand dollars. He tried to tell himself that it was merely coincidence; that the combination of too much rest and rich food was making his mind play tricks on him. But deep down, where a man hides his secret fears, the sleet of apprehension was already forming when Hook Hooligan came in and asked, "What'd Doc say about your leg?"

"Another day before I walk," Rennevant said.

Then he asked casually, "How long was Bob Cruzatte away from San Sabino?"

"Two, three months, as I recollect."

That information turned Rennevant thoughtful. It tallied with his forming suspicion. And it didn't please him. But he asked, "Where was he—in Texas?"

"Nope. Up north, Colorady and Wyoming."

Rennevant slowly built a smoke. There was one more question he had to ask; one final link of information that could kill the crawling thing inside him—that could banish the fantastic suspicion stirred into shape by Anne's mention of two thousand dollars. Even though the Faro Kid had stolen that exact amount of money from the Union Pacific—and had been hanging around Laramie gambling joints for about two months before the robbery—there was one more important link; one that had to do with a girl's oval face and light blond hair.

"Is Bob younger than Anne?" Rennevant asked.

"Nope," Hook said, some secret amusement twinkling in his eyes.

"How much older?" Rennevant inquired eagerly, hoping that the liveryman would say five years at least.

But Hook said, "He ain't no older. They're twins."

Whereupon Rennevant knew why Anne's face had seemed familiar that first night in the hallway.

The Faro Kid had the same kind of face—the same kind of eye and hair; the Faro Kid was Anne's twin brother!

The positive conviction that this was so—that the outlaw he'd trailed from Laramie to Cascabelle Divide was Bob Cruzatte—churned up a welter of emotion in Steve Rennevant. He'd seen the Faro Kid on numerous occasions in Laramie: a handsome, yellow-haired young blade who'd gambled every night, playing faro bank so consistently that the dealers had nicknamed him the Faro Kid. He had made several substantial wins. But there was a rashness in him that he didn't seem able to control, and so he had inevitably lost back most of his winnings.

Recalling that now, and knowing how surely he was the reckless son of a free-fighting father, Rennevant understood why the Faro Kid had held up a train—why he would hold up a dozen trains if the occasion called for it. Bob Cruzatte had been trying hard to get money to save Anvil!

But that didn't change the fact that the Kid was wanted in Wyoming. It didn't give a deputy marshal any excuse for deviating from the direct line of his duty. And neither did the fact that the finest, most beautiful girl in the world happened to be the Kid's sister. But it was enough to make a man curse the day he was born.

Hook asked, "Leg achin' ye, lad?"

Rennevant shook his head. There was an ache in him all right. But it wasn't in his leg.

"Ye look like ye need a drink," the old Irishman declared.

He went to the shelf and, reaching behind dusty bottles of horse liniment, produced a nearly full quart of *Colonel's Monogram*. "One long swig will fix anything up to and includin' cabin fever," he announced.

Rennevant took a swig. He said, "Thanks," and later he hobbled over to the shelf and took another.

There was, he reflected, no limit to the peculiar pranks Fate could play on a man. No limit at all.

Through most of that long afternoon Rennevant thought, and cursed, and made limping excursions to the whiskey bottle. Finally, when his leg began to ache, he brought the bottle to the cot. By the time Anne came with his supper, Rennevant was sleeping, fully dressed except for his boots. And the empty bottle was beside his gun on the blankets.

The first shock of knowing he was drunk—that he was capable of drinking himself into oblivion like any common saddle bum on a spree—held Anne in frowning contemplation. Not that she blamed a man for taking a drink, or several drinks, on occasion. But Steve had seemed above such weak and careless ways. Especially at a time like this, when his very life depended upon constant vigilance; when only the speed of his right hand might mean the difference between living and dying.

Sprawled there, with whiskey smell hovering over him like a symbol of surrender, he looked more helpless, somehow, than he'd looked that morning when she'd held the tourniquet tight above his wound. His haggard features had been taut then; even his bloodless lips had been firmly resolute, as if controlled by a fighting man's stiff, unbending pride. Steve didn't look proud now. All his features were relaxed, and there was a cynical, self-mocking grin on his loose-lipped mouth.

Anne hadn't cried that other time she'd found him lying here. And she didn't now. But she felt closer to it, and only Hook Hooligan's arrival caused her to hold back the bitter tears.

"Why did you give him that bottle?" she demanded, turning upon the old liveryman wrathfully.

Hook blinked. He stared at Rennevant and blinked again.

"I didn't think he'd guzzle the whole quart," he muttered. "He looked downright troubled, like mebbe his leg was givin' him misery. But he shouldn't of drank so much—not with them Double D spalpeens in town."

Anne put down the tray. She picked up Steve's gun and arranged the chair so that it faced the doorway. "I'll stay here until you do your chores," she said grimly. "Then it'll be your turn."

But half an hour later, when Hooligan came in to relieve her, Anne remembered his steel hook. "Can you shoot straight, left-handed?" she inquired.

"Not awful straight," he admitted. "But I couldn't miss a man in the doorway, which is as far as I'll have to shoot."

Whereupon Anne gave him Steve's gun and said, "I'll be back soon."

At the doorway she turned, giving Steve's sprawled, indistinct shape a lingering regard. And feeling closer to him, somehow, than she'd ever felt, she said softly, "Poor Steve."

Another day. Another afternoon of watching shadows slide past the barn doorway—and of dismal thinking. Rennevant kept remembering how graciously Anne had accepted his meagre apology for being asleep when she had brought his supper the night before. He guessed that she'd known he was drunk, but he didn't want her to know the reason for his spree. Not yet. Not until he'd looked at her brother Bob and knew beyond any doubt that he was the Faro Kid.

Rennevant became aware of footsteps on the plank sidewalk, coming that way. He listened intently, making his guess as to the walker's weight. A

ight man, he decided; but not Hook Hooligan, for
Hook was out in the corral exercising Rowdy—
getting the big sorrel ready for the long ride north.
And it wasn't Red Haggin, who'd weigh all of two
hundred pounds. It might be Whitey Hallmark,
though; made brave by Border Belle whiskey and
figuring to get his revenge against a bed-fast cripple,

Rennevant grinned. If it was Whitey, the Double
O ramrod had a surprise coming to him. A real surprise. Rennevant watched a man's shadow protrude
into the doorway and, scanning it closely, felt an
odd sense of disappointment. The shape of that
shadow made him lower his gun at once, for he'd
already recognized the tall pattern of Pete Modesto's
stovepipe hat when the old gambler stepped hurriedly inside.

Piano Pete wiped perspiration from his forehead.
He shook hands and asked wheezily, "How you feeling, friend Steve?"

"Mean," Rennevant muttered. "Downright mean."

Modesto glanced furtively behind him. He went
to the door and glanced out, then came close to the
cot and said, "There's something in the wind, Steve."

Rennevant grinned. "Usually is," he said, eyeing
Modesto thoughtfully; remembering what Hooligan
had said about Pete having a "case" on Kate Car-
nody. It occurred to Rennevant that Piano Pete had
always been a difficult man to understand. Even in
Cheyenne he'd seemed different from the tinhorn
bunch he'd worked with. He was like a man
prompted by cross purposes and complex impulses.

"I don't know what the deal is," Modesto said
whisperingly. "But there's something in the wind,
and it smells like a funeral for you."

"Every man is entitled to one funeral," Rennevant said, "and he's pretty damn certain to get one,
sooner or later."

Then he asked, "How did Diamond Dan take his trouncing? Does he show any signs of mending his greedy ways, at least until he can get another crew together?"

"Didn't seem to feaze him at all," Modesto said. "He's just as chesty as ever, and sticking to one drink a day, like always. But he's a born schemer, Steve—he's planning something right now. Something important. He's got Shumway, Hallmark and Haggin in his office. Been there over an hour."

"So?" Rennevant mused.

Modesto turned back to the door. "Keep your eyes peeled, especially after dark tonight," he warned, and went hurriedly outside.

Rennevant eased back on the cot, his imagination remotely stirred by the old gambler's talk. It occurred to him that this stable was a poor place to watch things; especially the back room, where he couldn't even get a look at the street. It was like being cooped up in a blind alley. So thinking, he pulled on his boots and limped out to the doorway bench. And presently, deciding that Doc Dineen was an overly cautious medico, he walked slowly to the hotel and asked Kate Carmody for a room.

Surprised, and pleased to see him able to navigate, she gave him the same room he'd had. When he passed Bob Cruzatte's closed door, Rennevant felt an urgent impulse to open it—to get the damn chore over and done with. But he heard Anne's voice in there, and so went quietly to his room.

Afterward, when he sat near the window, he saw Whitey Hallmark leave the saloon and walk to Matabelle's Mercantile. Five minutes later Diamond Dan Bannerman made a leisurely trip to the San Sabino Bank.

Watching the big saloon man, Rennevant tried to tally Bannerman's breed; accurately to judge his calibre against the time of showdown. Would Diamond Dan accept a challenge to shoot it out, man to man? Could his pride be used for a spur to prod him into a rash, unplanned conflict? Or would Bannerman wait until the odds were made to order—until he could call the plays himself?

Idly watching the sun-hammered street, Rennevant saw Bannerman walk back to the saloon. Shortly afterward Banker Kiley hurried over to Mabelle's Mercantile, and Rennevant was toying with the thought that there might be a definite pattern in these seemingly unrelated incidents, when he heard Anne leave her brother's room.

Waiting until she'd gone down the stairs, Rennevant hobbled along the hall. This, he told himself, was something he had to do. Wilfully marshaling his determination, he recalled that a thief had killed his father—and felt some of his old hate come back to him. The hate that had helped him attain his man-hunting reputation. Once a thief, always a thief, he told himself—and cursed the Faro Kid.

Stepping quietly to the open doorway, Rennevant saw Anne's brother, and stopped in momentary surprise. Bob Cruzatte, he knew instantly, was the Faro Kid; but he didn't look the same. Lying in bed, with a faint smile on his pale face and circles under his eyes, he didn't look like a train-robbing renegade at all. His blanched, bony face bore only slight resemblance now to the reckless, high-stake Faro Kid.

Cruzatte said, "Been expecting you, Rennevant. Come in, and close the door."

He motioned to a chair. "Thought I fooled you that day on Cascabelle Divide. But after what I hear about your siding my dad, I'm glad you followed me here."

Rennevant sat down. He said flatly, "You didn't miss fooling me by much. But you missed, and you're going back to face the music soon as you're able to ride."

"You seem awful sure about that," Cruzatte mused.

His slightly scoffing tone stirred a quick resentment in Rennevant. This brother of Anne's had plenty of brass.

Then Cruzatte said quietly, "I've got a favor to ask, badgetoter. Just a little favor."

Rennevant stood up. "You know the favors I give your kind," he muttered, and was turning toward the door when the sheet slipped away from Cruzatte's right hand, exposing a gun.

There was a bright glint in Cruzatte's eyes now, and a grin on his face that made him look more like the Faro Kid—like the rash gambler Rennevant had seen in Laramie. "Sit down," Cruzatte ordered, waggling the gun suggestively.

"No," Rennevant said. "I prefer to fight my snakes standing up."

Cruzatte's grin faded. His lips tightened into a thin line; desperate, deadly purpose flamed in his eyes. Because Steve Rennevant had seen this change come into many faces, he understood thoroughly what it meant. The Faro Kid was priming himself for a cold-turkey killing!

Cruzatte's thumb drew the hammer back, that slight click of cocking mechanism sounding sharp against the room's strict silence. Rennevant ignored the leveled gun; he watched Cruzatte's face, tautly waiting for some telltale sign that would give him a split-second warning. If he could anticipate the exact instant Cruzatte decided to release that hammer, there'd be a chance for a dodge-and-draw play then. A good chance. For the wounded renegade was still weak, and he was lying on his side, with his gun arm cramped awkwardly.

Excitement flushed Cruzatte's cheeks, and this flood of color emphasized his resemblance to Anne; a resemblance so striking now that it put a sudden reluctance into Rennevant. If he got a chance to send a slug at Bob Cruzatte it would seem almost like shooting at Anne.

With that thought chilling his habitual relish for conflict, Rennevant asked abruptly, "What was the favor?"

Relief showed instantly in Cruzatte's face. He lowered the gun's hammer and said, "Just a gentleman's agreement that you'll stay away from me for twenty-four hours after I'm able to walk—and that you won't tell anyone why we ride out of town together when the time comes."

"And if I say no?" Rennevant asked.

"Well, I've never killed in cold blood, but I'll kill you—before I'll let this town know why you trailed me here."

Rennevant eyed him narrowly. Bob Cruzatte, he decided, wasn't quite so tough as he made out. Still redfast, and facing inevitable imprisonment, Bob's thoughts were all for his loved ones—whom he wanted to protect from disgrace.

"All right," Rennevant said. "It's a deal."

Then he asked, "Do you know who stole your money?"

"Yeah, but I'm not telling. That's what I want the twenty-four hours for—to get it back."

"Mebbe I'll beat you to it," Rennevant suggested. "I've got a couple ideas on that score myself."

"You may not live long enough to do much looking," Cruzatte said cynically. "Which is why I'm not too much worried about your taking me back to Wyoming. You been lucky, up to now. But your luck might run out, Rennevant. You're living on borrowed time."

A mirthless smile twisted Rennevant's lips. "The last man told me that died with a bullet in his back," he said.

"Didn't know you did that kind of shooting," Cruzatte chided. Then, turning serious, he added, "Anne tells me you beat up Whitey Hallmark and bluffed Red Haggin into quitting like a yellow dog. She seems to think you've got a charmed life. But I know different, Rennevant. Bannerman's hired guns will get you in the end."

Remembering Modesto's warning, Rennevant said, "They might," and, going back to his room, took up his patient watching at the window. There was something in the wind, all right. There was heartbreak for Anne, when she found out about her brother being a thief. And she'd find out. For once Bob was convicted of the train robbery, the news would filter back to San Sabino and she'd know then why a drifting deputy marshal had ridden off with her brother instead of asking her to marry him.

Rennevant was still thinking about that, and feeling lower than he'd ever felt, when he went downstairs. Anne, he guessed, was in the kitchen preparing Bob's supper. Kate Carmody was playing the piano in the parlor. Rennevant glanced that way as he passed and saw Pete Modesto standing beside Kate with an expression on his face that Rennevant had never glimpsed before: an expression of exuberant happiness that bordered on ecstasy—that softened Modesto's gaunt features and put a prideful glow in the gambler's eyes.

Rennevant walked on out to the veranda unobserved. Piano Pete, he decided, had more than just a "case" on Kate. The man worshipped the air she breathed!

10

Walking slowly, Rennevant crossed the street, after eating supper at Estevan's Cafe. It was full dark now and the chances of being noticed seemed trivial yet the opportunity for ambush on this dimly lighted street was a definite threat and it turned him warily alert as he limped to the Cattle King.

He went up the hotel steps and, hearing Anne call his name from the far end of the veranda, knew instantly that something was wrong.

When he joined her on the bench she said, "Dan Bannerman has threatened Matabelle. He told Tate Kiley that Matabelle is doomed—unless he quits backing the Pool at once."

Expecting something entirely different—that she had somehow found out about Bob—Rennevant loosed a sigh of relief. He lit his after-supper cigar and said presently, "It may be just a bluff, Anne. Bannerman knows he can't whip the Pool with the crew he has left, and that it'll take considerable time to replace the gunslick bunch he lost. So he wants to do it the easy way—by starving the Pool out. He's probably putting the pressure on Kiley to foreclose those mortgages, and trying to spook Matabelle at the same time."

Then he asked, "Is Matabelle going to quit?"

"No, he's not quitting. But I don't think Bannerman is bluffing." She glanced up at the lights on Society Hill and said, "I'd hate to see anything happen to Mayor John. He's the only real hope this town has—or the whole basin, for that matter."

But Rennevant couldn't keep his thoughts away

from the Faro Kid. Each time he looked at Anne he saw the brash image of her twin brother; the image of the thief he was going to arrest. A faint bloom of window lamplight revealed Anne's profile, and the blond loveliness of her hair. Her features, so like Bob's were more gently moulded, the angles of cheek and chin less severe. But her hair, even though it was of a finer texture, was the exact shade of the Faro Kid's hair.

Anne said presently, "A *centavo* for your thoughts, Steve."

Remembering the other time she had said that, Rennevant smiled reflectively. It seemed a long time ago. Many things had happened since then. Too damned many. They'd been on their way up Sashay Ridge, and everything had been simple, compared to now. Soon after she'd said those words he'd kissed her, for the first time.

"Two *centavos*, then," she prompted.

"I was remembering Sashay Ridge," he admitted "Reckon I'll always remember it."

Anne smiled. Her fingers found his hand and gently pressed it, and she whispered, "I wish you would, Steve."

Exactly as she'd said it that day. With the same sweet urgency in her voice; the same slow smile on her lips.

Rennevant took her into his arms, holding her so that he could see the shadow-veiled oval of her face He wanted to look into her eyes while he told her what he had to tell, and dreaded telling.

He said, "Anne."

He thought for words to explain why he had no right, now, to her affection. But he couldn't find the words. And in that moment, while she waited for his kiss, Steve Rennevant tried to beat down the impulse that reared inside him. He told himself that she wouldn't be offering him her lips if she knew he was going to arrest Bob. She'd be hating him with a bitter, unreasoning hate; and remembering that she'd once saved him from Red Haggin's gun out there on Main Street, she'd regret that day as long as she lived.

But even with that knowledge slogging through his mind, he couldn't tell her. And he couldn't resist those smiling, half-parted lips. Even though he felt like a sneaking fraud, he kissed her; long and hard. Like a farewell kiss. And that, he told himself, was what it was to be—one lingering, sweet scented farewell to a fabulous dream. To a dream that could never come true.

For a timeless interval then, while she lay quietly in his arms, Rennevant fought a second battle with himself. A brutal, infinitely more urgent battle, that had no alternative save shame and self-disgust. For even though he had intended to quit the law game, and still intended to, he'd be welching on his sworn duty if he turned in his badge simply to dodge the chore of arresting Bob Cruzatte. He'd be in the same class with Fay Shumway, and all the other grafting fakes who made a mockery of law and order—who dealt out their own brand of personal justice as it suited their needs.

Yet this girl in his arms meant so much to him.

Anne stirred, and glanced through the window at the lobby clock. "Good heavens!" she exclaimed. "You've made me forget my duties as a nurse. I've got to give Bob his medicine."

Rennevant walked with her to the doorway, trying not to limp; not wanting her to know that his leg still bothered him.

She said, "I'll be down in a little while, Steve. Wait for me."

"All right," he agreed and, watching her go up

the stairs, realized how monstrously Fate had tricked them both.

Grimly, as a man contemplating each turn in a twisted, one-way trail, Rennevant reviewed the circumstances which had brought him a thousand miles to stand here with the flavor of a girl's passionate kiss upon his lips. A man's destiny, he reflected, was shaped by damned peculiar things—by half-filled canteens and queer old gamblers, and a girl's mention of two thousand dollars. For all those things had led inevitably to this moment.

Turning back across the veranda, Rennevant glanced at the Border Belle's batwings. Maybe a drink was what he needed now. Maybe a glass of bourbon would cure the sudden sense of futility which was growing like a cold knot inside him. It had been bad enough before, knowing that he'd have to arrest Anne's twin brother. But now, with her kiss still warm and fragrant on his lips, the part he was playing seemed like a Judas role.

He went down the steps and, recalling Piano Pete's warning to watch out after dark, wished savagely that Bannerman's gunhawks would start something tonight. A fight was what he needed now. A damned good fight, and a drink.

And at that exact moment a man in front of Matabelle's Mercantile yelled, "*Fire!*"

An orange glow showed behind the Mercantile's front windows, and the smell of smoke was already tainting the air. Men rushed into the street, quickly forming a crowd that surged against Rennevant and forced him back against the hotel veranda.

The bell atop the courthouse began bonging out its alarm, and a man yelled, "Come on—come on! Bucket brigade!"

The fire, Rennevant reckoned, was in the rear of the store. No flame showed above the building's tall false front, but when a hastily formed bucket brigade forced the front door open, a great cloud of smoke billowed out into the street.

Recalling what Anne had told him a few minutes before, Rennevant guessed why the fire had been started. It could be concidence, of course, and no one could prove it wasn't; but it looked like something else. It looked like Dan Bannerman's method of blocking opposition.

Rennevant moved slowly along the street, favoring his bad leg. He stood at the edge of the smoke-draped ineffectual efforts against the crackling flames. Presently Mayor Matabelle shouldered his way through the throng and shouted, "Close that door! Bring your water around back!"

The old merchant grasped a bucket from another man's hands and disappeared into the narrow passageway which skirted his store. The bucket line was quickly reformed, and the first pail of water was being handed along when the sharp blast of a gun sounded above the crackle of flames.

Then a man shouted: "Matabelle's been shot!"

The gun blasted again, fired from somewhere behind the store, and a panic-stricken voice screeched, "Let me out of here!"

The rest of it was bedlam of noise and confusion. Men rushed from the smoke-fogged alley like stampeded steers. A woman called frantically, "Frank—Frank!"

Watching all this with the calm detachment of a man who'd seen violence in many towns, Rennevant saw Diamond Dan Bannerman standing at the far edge of the crowd with his fat bartender. They seemed unimpressed, untouched by the turmoil about them. Then Rennevant turned his attention to Sheriff Shumway, who strode into the alley, followed by Doc Dineen.

The rear portion of the store was now a roaring inferno, the heat of its forward surging flames forcing the crowd back. Rennevant glimpsed Tate Kiley, standing with his wife and another stylishly garbed woman. When Doc Dineen came out of the alley and said, "Mayor John is dead," Kiley's worried face turned a ghastly gray and the woman began sobbing hysterically.

Seeing these things, Rennevant understood how ruthlessly Dan Bannerman had eliminated opposition to his plan to starve out the Pool. Matabelle's murder meant more than the loss of financial backing; it would serve as a threatening club to force Banker Kiley into submission—into foreclosing the mortgages on those ranches in the Homestead Hills.

Rennevant turned back toward the hotel and had taken a dozen steps when he met Anne. She said, "Isn't it awful?" and took his arm.

Rennevant nodded. "There'll be no food or ammunition for the fight against Bannerman now."

"I'm not thinking of that," Anne said, "I'm thinking of poor Mrs. Matabelle—and those five families who'll lose their homes. Tate Kiley will be afraid to refuse Bannerman's proposition now. Tate will do what he's told, and so will everyone else in this town."

"Yes," Rennevant agreed, and felt a high surge of admiration at her swift sympathy for others.

Nearing the hotel, Rennevant glanced across at the Border Belle and, recalling that he'd seen the white-aproned barkeep at the fire with Bannerman, had a sudden inspiration. If Double D riders had taken the two thousand dollars from Bob Cruzatte, the money would probably be cached in the big man's office; in his desk, perhaps—or a safe. And the Border Belle was deserted.

Deciding it was worth a try, Rennevant said, "Excuse me, Anne. I'm going to have a looksee at the lion's den."

Whereupon he left her and was crossing the street when she called softly, "Be careful, Steve."

But her voice was lost in the noise of the fire, and Rennevant didn't hear her. Limping to the saloon, he crossed the stoop and stepped inside. The long room was deserted, the door to Bannerman's office closed. Glancing back to the street, Rennevant saw Red Haggin and Whitey Hallmark ride up Main Street, and that puzzled him. There'd been no doubt in his mind as to who had set the fire and shot Matabelle. If these two had been out of town—

Then he guessed how they had worked it. They'd forted up behind the store, shot Matabelle and then ridden a wide circle, making it appear as if they'd just ridden in from the ranch.

He saw two men carry Matabelle's lifeless body out of the alley while Sheriff Shumway opened a lane for them through the milling crowd. People still converged on the fire from all directions, their excited voices merging with the roar of rising flames.

A mirthless smile creased Rennevant's face. San Sabino's attention was completely centered over here; a man could shoot the lock off a safe here without detection.

Rennevant eased the office door open, thumbed a match into flame and went to the safe beside Bannerman's desk. The safe door was partly open, this discovery causing him to guess there was no money in it. Diamond Dan wouldn't be so careless with two thousand dollars.

It was a matter of minutes, and five more matches, until Rennevant had thoroughly ransacked the safe and was out in Border Belle Alley—empty-handed. He walked around to Main Street and found Anne awaiting him on the hotel veranda.

"Have your looksee?" she asked, a plain note of relief in her voice.

Rennevant nodded. "But I didn't find what I was looking for."

Glancing at the fire, he saw that the Mercantile's roof had fallen in. Smoke hung in wavering streamers all along the street, carrying the pungent odors of burnt coffee and onions and dry goods. But only a broad bed of glowing coals remained where the store had stood an hour before.

The crowd was breaking up. Men tromped the board sidewalks, discussing the mayor's murder and the mysterious fire which had preceded it. Few of them would guess the portent of this night's tragic occurrences, and the few who did would not divulge their suspicions. More than ever now, San Sabino would be a place of fear; of furtive watching and hushed waiting. For a time tonight the brooding expectancy had been banished by the excitement of the fire. But now the flames had dwindled to smouldering embers and a corpse lay on a slab at Slocum's Undertaking Parlor. Fear would ride this mayorless town like a shroud; it would be a withering plague to sap men's courage.

As if sharing these thoughts, Anne said, "There's not a chance for the Anvil now. But Dad won't quit."

Then she added softly, "I'll not hold you to our bargain, Steve. Your help would only prolong the misery. It wouldn't save us, and it might cost you your life. I wouldn't want that to happen."

Sadness was in her subdued voice. And a kind of hopeless futility. But no complaint; no protesting the loss of all her high hope. She was, Rennevant reflected, a fit daughter for a fighting father; a Viking's daughter. Come hell or high water, she would stand shoulder to shoulder with Jeff Cruzatte. And Jeff would fight until the last rasping breath ran out of him.

"Our bargain holds," Rennevant drawled, and then he asked, "Remember what I said that night on the gallery—about there being no real peace in this country until Bannerman left it?"

Anne nodded. "And you said there was only one way he'd leave it."

"Well," Rennevant said, "mebbe I could take care of that tonight, with a little luck."

Anne grasped his arm. "You're in no shape to fight," she exclaimed. "It wouldn't be just Bannerman—you'd have to fight Shumway and Hallmark and Haggin. If only Dad and the others were here to help you—"

Then a new thought struck her, and she said, "I'm going to get them, Steve! I'm going to ride out there and find them—right now!"

"Better wait till morning," he counselled. "You might have to do considerable looking."

But Anne wouldn't listen. "I'm going to borrow Kate's riding togs, and tell Bob where I'm going," she declared, hurrying into the hotel.

Ten minutes later Rennevant walked with her to the livery, not liking to have her go alone, yet knowing what so long a ride would do to his wounded leg. Just before she rode away, Anne said urgently, "Promise you won't go gunning for Bannerman until Dad and the others get here, Steve."

"Promise," he agreed, whereupon she rode down Main Street at a run.

On his way back to the hotel, Rennevant stopped at the post office and, getting the letter he'd been waiting for, read it eagerly. It said:

"Only Hallmark and Red Haggin still at large. These men wanted, dead or alive, for murder while robbing United States mail."

Rennevant grinned. Hallmark and Haggin. Two
killer thieves who needed hanging. Then he remembered that the Faro Kid was also wanted. There'd
been a time when the chance to capture three
thieves would have filled him with anticipation;
when the opportunity to carve a triple notch of revenge on his father's tombstone would have whipped
up a savage eagerness. But not now—not with Anne's
twin brother included in that trio.

Rennevant limped back to the hotel and sat down.
Pete Modesto was talking to Kate Carmody in the
lobby; something about music. Strange, that these
two should have that common bond of interest. A
tin-horn gambler and a girl half his age. Kate, he
guessed, was unaware of Modesto's intense attach-
ment for her; probably had no suspicion that his interest went beyond teaching her how to play the
piano. Far beyond—

Then Rennevant saw Fat Foster come across the
street, white apron jiggling to his ponderous stride.
The big-bellied barkeep came up the steps and went
into the hotel like a man on an important mission.

Stepping over to the open window, Rennevant
watched Foster hand Modesto a battered gold watch
—heard him say bluntly, "Dan says he knows a
girl who looks like the picture in the back of this
thing. He wants to see you—right away."

Modesto's gaunt face went chalky. A look of panic
came into his eyes, and for a moment he stood staring at the watch. Then he said, "All right, Fat," and
accompanied Foster back across the street.

Rennevant walked to the steps and stood there
for a moment, trying to figure it out. Part of it was
plain to him. The battered watch had broken the
saloon's front chandelier that first night. But the
part about the girl's picture was a puzzle he couldn'
solve. And if Bannerman had known it was Pete'

watch, why had he waited all this time to accuse the gambler of its ownership?

Kate came out of the lobby and asked, "What in the world were they talking about?"

Rennevant shrugged. "I don't know," he muttered, going down the steps. "But I aim to find out."

"Oh, you mustn't go over there!" the girl cautioned. "Bob says they're just waiting for a chance to kill you!"

That earnest admonition brought a cynical smile to Rennevant's lips. Kate Carmody would be another one who'd hate him when the news got back that Bob was in prison.

He crossed Main Street and, going down Border Belle Alley, reached the rear of the saloon. Then he eased over to where a window of Bannerman's office made a yellow daub of light and, peering through a corner of dust-begrimed glass, saw something that made him blink his eyes.

Piano Pete stood in front of Bannerman's desk —taking a compact bundle of bills from the front of his unbuttoned shirt!

Utterly astonished, Rennevant watched the old gambler's trembling hands deposit four neatly wrapped bundles on the desk; four bundles marked $500—and knew instantly that this was the money Bob Cruzatte had stolen from the Union Pacific!

Rennevant couldn't see Bannerman from this angle, but he could hear the big man's gloating voice. "I wasn't sure it was you grabbed that bankroll," Bannerman declared. "But I knew the watch would spook you into admitting it, if you did."

Vaguely, like a man stunned into dazed submission, Modesto mumbled, "It wasn't the watch. It was the picture inside it."

Bannerman loosed a slow, dribbling chuckle. "That picture cost you two thousand dollars," he taunted. "It may cost you your thieving hide before I get through with you."

"Don't care about that," Modesto muttered. "Just so you leave Kate alone."

That declaration puzzled Rennevant. It didn't seem possible that one man could possess such contrasting characteristics. Piano Pete must be some sort of saint-and-sinner fanatic. But even though Rennevant couldn't comprehend Modesto's tangled motives, he felt no less obligated to the old gambler. In fact, he felt a sort of pity for him.

Rennevant drew his gun. Here was a chance to save Modesto, and recover the Union Pacific's stolen funds at the same time. And if Bannerman tried to stop him, there'd be a chance to end all the trouble in Kettledrum Basin—with one well-aimed shot.

Easing over to the door, Rennevant felt for the latch. Bannerman was still talking; still gloating. His desk was near this door; so near he'd be almost within arm's length once the door was opened.

"Beginning tonight I'm running this town my way," Bannerman bragged. "Anybody that don't like it better move out goddam fast."

Rennevant thumbed back the hammer of his gun. He reached for the latch with his left hand, hoping urgently that the door wasn't locked. And at that exact instant a gun blasted behind him!

11

THAT FIRST SLUG slammed into the door frame close enough to make Rennevant dodge. He whirled and saw muzzle flame stab the clotted shadows of a

wagon yard across the alley and heard another bullet whang past him. He snapped a shot that way,
ducked off the stoop and, crouching behind a trash
barrel, saw the light fade from Bannerman's window.

For a long moment then there was absolute
silence. Smoke still trailed on the windless air in fog-
like streamers, dimming the faint glimmer of a cres-
cent moon. Rennevant probed the yonder shadows;
wondered who his attacker was. Red Haggin, or
Whitey Hallmark, he guessed. Whoever it was, the
dirty son had tried to shoot him in the back, and
hadn't missed by much. That realization put a savage eagerness into Rennevant—a familiar, itching
urge for conflict. He slanted a shot into the wagon
yard and, ignoring a spray of splinters from a slug-
smashed barrel stave, fired at the answering muzzle
flare.

His shot was instantly echoed by a high-pitched
curse. He glimpsed a blur of movement between two
wagons, fired again, and saw a man dodge back into
the deeper shadows of a shed. Rennevant went
across the alley in a limping run, hunkered behind
a heavy gate post and was scanning the jumble of
wagons and rubbish that littered the yard, when
Bannerman's demanding voice came from somewhere behind him. "Who's out there?"

Rennevant stood rigidly still against the post.
There was a long moment of silence, and in that
hushed interval, a drone of excited talk drifted down
from Main Street. Then a shrill voice called, "It's
me, Whitey—and I got Rennevant cornered!"

Rennevant grinned, highly pleased that it was
Hallmark out there ahead of him; Whitey Hallmark,
who was wanted—dead or alive. Here was a chance
to do what he'd wanted to do that first day out on
the stage road!

There was no further word from Bannerman, and

that omission rang a bell of warning in Rennevant's brain. Diamond Dan, he guessed, was already organizing a flank attack that would close a trap behind him. It occurred to Rennevant that there was still time to run out of there. He could cut across that back street and circle through the residential district over there in comparative safety. But this was a law job and it needed doing right now.

Using the Double D ramrod's voice for a target, Rennevant sent three fast shots at the shed and ran into the wagon yard. Hallmark fired twice, both those slugs snarling close. Rennevant dropped behind a stack of corded firewood, stopping long enough to pluck fresh shells from his belt and reload. Then he ran around the woodpile in a stooped zigzag charge.

Hallmark's gun boomed again, and that bullet scorched a prickling furrow across Rennevant's cheek. But because he'd kept a strict tally on Hallmark's firing, Rennevant grinned as he rushed the wagon shed. Whitey had fired five times. Unless he used a six-shell load—which was unlikely—Hallmark's gun was empty.

And at that moment, as Rennevant glimpsed a motion-blurred shape drifting around the shed's far corner, guns blasted from the alley. Lead laced the air around him as he dove headlong beneath a high-wheeled freighter. Bullets kept striking metal parts of the wagon, *pinging* crazily in ricochet; they crashed through splintering wood and plunked into the shed's adobe wall. Rennevant swiveled around on his stomach and, seeing shadowy shapes converge at the gateway, raked that vague opening with five slugs.

Hastily reloading, he heard Sheriff Shumway call, "Where are you, Whitey?"

And from somewhere off to the left, Dan Banner-